## PRAISE FOR ROBYN BACHAR'S BAD WITCH SERIES

This is a wonderfully imaginative tale that begs a re-read just so that every detail and nuance can be savored.

— *RT BOOK REVIEWS*, 4 1/2 STAR REVIEW FOR *THE IMPORTANCE OF BEING EMILY*

*Blood, Smoke and Mirrors* contains all the things I love the best in books, great internal and external tension, quirky or slightly flawed protagonists, great dialogue, and a captivating story line.

— *LONG AND SHORT ROMANCE REVIEWS*, 5 BOOK REVIEW

I am seriously recommending that you read this book if you want something to distract you from anything and everything on your mind. The world painted in this book is such a great one to escape to that I literally could not put it down.

— *NIGHT OWL REVIEWS*, 5 STAR TOP PICK REVIEW FOR *BEWITCHED, BLOODED AND BEWILDERED*

FIRE IN THE BLOOD is a sizzling, suspenseful paranormal romance.

— *FRESH FICTION*

BAD BLOOD



This book is a work of fiction. The names, characters, places, and incidents are products of the writer's imagination or have been used fictitiously and are not to be construed as real. Any resemblance to persons, living or dead, actual events, locale or organizations is entirely coincidental.

Robyn Bachar

P.O. Box 1692

Riverside IL 60546

Editing by Deborah Nemeth

Cover by Kanaxa

Ebook ISBN: 978-0-9963490-9-3

Print ISBN: 978-1-7335761-1-6



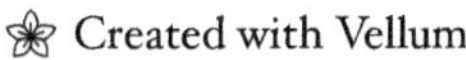

# BAD BLOOD

Bad Witch Book 5

ROBYN BACHAR

# ACKNOWLEDGMENTS

Special thanks go to my editor Deb Nemeth, who makes me a better author with every book we work together on.

I'd like to thank BFF Diana, Jim, Sasha, Karrin, and David, who encourage me to never give up. I am eternally grateful for your support.

And to my family, for their continued love and support. I am blessed to have you.

# CONTENTS

# CHAPTER ONE

*Are you taking readings?*

I frowned at Piper's text before firing off a reply.

*No. Do I bother you guys when you're working?* I added an emoji that cheerfully flipped her off for emphasis and considered the matter closed until my phone buzzed again.

*John wants you to use the Spirit Seekers app.*

I sighed. The app was a cute bit of fan service, but it didn't do much other than record audio for potential EVPs—electronic voice phenomenon, the whispers that paranormal investigators claimed were the voices of the dead.

I didn't believe in ghosts. I just worked for people who do. Irritating people who enjoyed texting me every five seconds.

*Too much noise contamination*, I replied. *I'm surrounded by loud British tourists.*

*Spirit Seekers* had wrapped production on its fourth season and John, the head investigator, was hungry to line up bigger, scarier sites for season five. Unfortunately, the Castillo de la Coracera didn't look haunted. Few locations did during daylight hours, though the gunmetal sky heralding an approaching thunderstorm added a gothic menace to the Castillo's silhouette. It loomed above the surrounding neighborhood like a warning—a grim reminder of times past.

If it were up to the team they'd investigate every crumbling, asbestos-riddled structure that was rumored to be haunted, but thankfully the network didn't allow that. It's my job to scout for photogenic locations with the right combination of intriguing normal and supernatural history. Right now the view was too monotone for film—good for a noir murder mystery, but not for our purposes. It also didn't help that the Castillo was miles away from the Disney-fied castles that *Spirit Seekers'* viewing audience expected. The American idea of a castle was one of picturesque drama and fantasy, a confection of delicate towers and soft colors crowned with a nightly fireworks display, and not the reality of a squat, bulldog fortification meant to repel enemy armies.

I traded my phone for my tablet and took notes to send to the team (and more importantly to the producers) as I toured the site. The Castillo's pamphlets claimed that visitors to the castle heard screams in the chapel and disembodied voices, and had witnessed floating rocks and the apparition of a ghostly soldier. Disembodied voices in a structure with questionable acoustics that was surrounded by modern civilization hardly seemed supernatural to me. And dislodged rocks in an old stone building? Please. Though the soldier did break my heart a bit. I'd visited a half dozen forts up and down America's east coast for the show, each with tales of resident unknown soldiers who diligently patrolled the walls after death. I didn't believe in ghosts, but I believed in honoring our armed forces, and there was power in the image of a soul so faithful to the cause that even death couldn't stop him from performing his duty.

Ultimately, the Castillo didn't scream *Spain*, and Spain was the reason I'd come here. Americans wanted sun-drenched Spanish villas with matadors in red capes—I knew, because I'd been expecting that myself. No luck so far, but I hadn't seen much of Madrid yet aside from the airport and my hotel. I had nine days in Madrid, and hopefully I'd find something with stronger visual interest. There had to be a haunted bullfighting ring somewhere. I also had leads on three different bars that Hemingway was said to haunt.

After two hours of compiling photos and notes, I headed back to my hotel, tapping an anxious beat on the steering wheel of my rented car. The drive didn't make me jittery—I feared no foreign traffic after spending a summer in Mexico City. Instead I was eager to meet with the local genealogist I'd hired. I'd been compiling our family tree as part of my parents' thirty-fifth wedding anniversary present. I dashed up to my room, changed out of my tourist attire, dragged a brush through my hair and hurried downstairs to meet my genealogist in the hotel's restaurant for tapas and wine. My stomach growled in eager anticipation—tapas had officially become my new favorite thing, but the small portion sizes mystified me. I'd always been what my mother diplomatically called "a good eater," as could be attested to by the generous plump to my ass and thickness of my thighs. I refused to travel the world and only order salads and diet sodas. My doctor gave me a clean bill of health, and until he says otherwise my motto is that life is too short to say no to butter. Or olive oil, in this case. The majority of the tapas I'd encountered thus far featured mystery seafood sautéed in olive oil, accompanied by olives, chunks of crusty bread and slices of goat cheese.

Señor Jorge Ramos was a grandfatherly gentleman with salt-and-pepper hair who was semi-retired. Genealogy was good business—I freelanced on occasion because my history degrees paired well with ancestry research. A person who knew where to look could access scanned documents from anywhere in the world, allowing nostalgic Americans to trace our roots back to whatever Old Country had birthed us. My schedule had been too busy to do this particular research myself, and having a local professional do the research was worth every euro. This was the *perfect* anniversary gift—thoughtful, thorough, and the ultimate proof that I valued family. It wasn't enough to free me from the prodigal daughter doghouse, but it was a giant leap in that direction.

Sr. Ramos smiled and rose. "Señorita Houlihan. I am so pleased to finally meet you." We shook hands, awkwardly—did the Spanish kiss each other's cheeks like the French? I was jetlagged and I hadn't been here long enough to notice the local customs.

"Please, call me Nati." I returned his smile and waved him to his seat. His accent was odd—I'm fluent in Spanish but I was struggling with the local accents. It sounded as though everyone spoke with a lisp, or maybe the whole country had a head cold.

I was so eager to hear his findings that I nearly bounced up and down in my chair like a caffeinated six-year-old kid, but I forced myself to be patient. We ordered a lovely bottle of red wine and I asked him about local historical sites of interest. I explained my work for the World History Channel and he paused, a bite of fried goat cheese hovering between his plate and his mouth.

"*¿Fantasmas?*" he repeated. *Ghosts* sounded much cooler in Spanish but no less embarrassing.

My cheeks burned and I giggled a nervous laugh. Most people looked at me like I was insane when they heard that I worked for *Spirit Seekers*. I dreaded that look.

"I know. I don't believe in ghosts, but it pays the bills." No amount of blurry "light anomalies" and grainy shadows the team presented as evidence convinced me of the existence of an afterlife.

Sr. Ramos cleared his throat. "You are not religious?"

"No, but my parents are." After being traumatized by Catholicism I swore off religion, which was one of the many points of contention between me and my mother.

"It is strange that you would mention ghosts, considering what I found."

"Oh?" A morbid chill raised goose bumps across my arms—that was not the transition I'd been expecting.

Sr. Ramos reached for his portfolio and withdrew a manila folder. I nearly drooled at the sight of it and folded my hands atop my linen napkin to fight the urge to snatch his findings up. He set the top page between us and unfolded it, revealing my family tree.

Generations of my ancestors were recorded in neat black font and connected with precise straight lines. Decades of history and entire lifetimes boiled down into name, date of birth and death, annotated with tiny superscript numbers. *Ooh. End notes.* I nearly squealed with joy—the good stuff was always hidden in the end notes, like academic Easter eggs.

"Here." Sr. Ramos tapped a cluster dated in the late 1600s. "It seemed unremarkable at first. One of many quiet generations who lived out their lives peacefully. Yet in searching for the name I came across this news article dated nearly two hundred years later." He produced a scanned, printed copy of the article in question. "It was written during the height of the spiritualist movement and describes a séance. It claims that the sister of your ancestor here"—he tapped the branch again"—was murdered, and her soul was not at rest."

"Murdered?" My jaw dropped and I picked up my wineglass, rolling the stem between my fingers. Sure I hoped for something surprising to tell my parents, but this wasn't what I had in mind.

"Yes. I will let you read it for yourself. It is quite dramatic, though everywhere in Spain is reputed to be haunted by some tragedy or other." Sr. Ramos waved a dismissive hand and shrugged. "I have not come across any other sources that specifically mention the incident, and there was no record of the cause of Angela's death."

Angela. My focus returned to the spot in question on the family tree and the name with no descendants. Angela's brother had married and had three children, one of whom connected all the way to me. Angela was a branch who never flowered, and she had been murdered at the tender age of eighteen. Being thirty-three suddenly made me feel positively ancient. My mom had been married at eighteen, and thankfully my dad's disapproving family had confined their disapproval to words and not weapons. I narrowly avoided being married at eighteen myself.

I cleared my throat and changed the subject. "What else did you find?"

We pored over pages of information—baptismal records and census data for the most part, mixed with obituaries and other newspaper announcements. Still no royal connections, but apparently in the 1600s my ancestors had been wealthy merchants who dealt in New World trade, doubtless at the expense of the Native Americans.

After another glass of wine I traded the payment for Sr. Ramos's work for the file. I hurried back to my room with my new treasure and spread the contents of the folder across the bed. The somber black-and-white photos fascinated me. My studies had taught me that the stoic expressions featured in early photography were not due to the burden of wearing ten pounds of fancy dress, complete with complicated undergarments, but instead were a result of the photo's long exposure time. Essentially it hurt to hold a smile for five minutes straight. Dark-haired men and women frowned at the camera, their names and pertinent information typed at the bottom of the printouts. Where were the originals? Must be in a library somewhere, or a historical society collection. I picked up the printout of a newspaper article.

Famous, or perhaps infamous, spiritualist medium Doña Marisol de la Vega conducted a séance on the evening of October 31st at midnight at the request of the grieving lady of the house, Doña Isabel García Parra. Having recently lost both children to cholera, Doña Isabel was anxious to contact the spirits of her loved ones.

Ouch. Life before modern medicine was hard, and losing both children at once? Damn. I'd be desperate enough to do anything, too... Well, probably not desperate enough to turn to an infamous spiritualist medium. Doña Marisol probably had one hand out to offer comfort while the other picked the grieving mother's pocket. Scowling, I moved on.

Doña Marisol was unable to contact the deceased children. Instead, she came across a spirit claiming to be one Angela Rodríguez de Mendoza, a young woman who told a tragic tale of murder. Slain on her wedding night by the jealous lover of her new husband, Angela's soul is unable to find rest. The forlorn spirit pleaded for aid until the medium was overcome by her exertions.

I snorted. Yeah, right. More likely she required more money to continue the reading. "For the bargain price of $19.95 you can continue the reading and save this poor damned soul." Where had Marisol gotten Angela's name? Maybe she'd trolled cemeteries, looking for crumbling tombstones and taking note of people who had died young. An eighteen-year-old bride would invoke sympathy, and the vicious jilted lover was a pretty standard trope. Though really I couldn't imagine being so worked up over a man that I'd kill for him. Plenty of fish in the sea, and I was an experienced fisher of men...

Angela had to be buried nearby. It would be a nice touch to the family tree if I visited her grave and took photos of her headstone, or any other residents of the family plot. I could chalk it up as a business expense if the network was interested in following this lead. I fired up my laptop and dashed off an email to Sr. Ramos thanking him for the excellent work and a lovely evening and asking if he knew the location of any local cemeteries where my ancestors were buried.

I needed to know what happened to her. Mama claimed that my first word was *why*, and I believed it. I'd always been consumed by curiosity, and never afraid to dig for answers. I loved it, in fact. I was happiest when surrounded by old documents, my gloved fingertips tracing words written decades, sometimes centuries ago. It was like reaching through time to touch history. I needed to know Angela's story, because it was part of our story—and anything that distracted my mother from my own story was well worth any effort.

The team seldom investigated cemeteries. As they explained it, cemeteries were for the living, not the dead—a place for grieving friends and family to visit and remember their loved ones. I supposed there was some sense in that, because I wouldn't want to hang out in a cemetery if I were a ghost. I'd want to be where I was most comfortable and had fond memories of. Or somewhere fun, like Disney World or Las Vegas.

Sr. Ramos had informed me that Angela's grave was located outside Barcelona. At first I'd assumed that the distance took visiting them off my itinerary, but the team wanted me to go. I'd emailed Piper a translation of the article about Angela's restless spirit, and she replied with an all-caps excited email and dove into the investigation. She loved a challenge, and the boys thanked me for distracting her from endlessly searching baby name sites. I tried explaining that despite their American assumption that all of Europe is tiny and everything is just next door, Madrid and Barcelona are not close and taking the train there and back would eat up a day of my trip, but the team was excited by the possible ratings bump of investigating a location that I had a personal tie to, so off I went.

A local associate who owed Sr. Ramos a favor had provided me with the cemetery's location. There's something poignantly melancholy about cemeteries—the stoic memorials, faded by years of sun, wind and rain. Generations who had passed from memory, with only a date and a name to remind the living of who had come before. Uncovering those forgotten stories had drawn me to study history. My mother claimed that I suffered from an overabundance of busibodiness and had gone into a profession that paid me to crawl around people's attics and uncover their dirty laundry in forgotten diaries and packets of old letters tied together with crumbling string. It was true enough, though to be fair now I also judged whether that dirty laundry was photogenic enough to be broadcast to the world in high definition.

The sculptures in the cemetery creeped me out. Weeping angels and mournful Madonnas guarded the graves, and I shivered and huddled deeper into my hoodie. I should've worn a sweater under it—I was never truly prepared for local weather no matter how much I agonized over weather reports and wardrobe choices.

I probably also should have grabbed an umbrella, judging by the fat gray clouds lumbering in this direction—the rain had followed me from Madrid like a stalker ex. I kept a rain poncho in my bag as a last resort, but it looked dorky and was awkward to wear. I didn't want to be mistaken for a bright yellow ghost trudging among the tombstones.

My canvas shoes were quickly soaked and stained green as I hurried through the damp, unkempt grass toward the spot on the map that promised to contain the graves of my distant relatives. I frowned at a tiny headstone, the timespan between birth and death only a handful of days. My eyes stung and I swallowed hard.

I didn't have children, and I intended to keep it that way. As the eldest of seven, I'd done my share of childcare while looking after my younger siblings. When I moved out I'd vowed that I would never share a bathroom with anyone ever again. My space was mine and mine alone. I could pick up and travel anywhere at a moment's notice, no babysitters, pet sitters or even plant sitters required. My father called me a free spirit, but my mother simply shook her head at my choices and looked forlorn. I kept hoping that once she reached a certain number of grandchildren she'd give up on me, but thus far she was focused on seeing her firstborn properly married.

A winding, overgrown path wove through the plots, and it led me away from the densely packed dead and onto a lane of stately mausoleums. After I passed the crypts, the trees thickened and the path led into unbeaten territory. I was sure I was headed the right way, but I checked my phone to make sure I still had a signal and functional GPS. I was a city dweller, and I didn't trust the outdoors. Who knew what local wildlife could be lurking in there? Creepy Spanish squirrels? Giant, bullfighting insects? I steeled my nerves and walked into the trees.

The path narrowed and was nearly devoured by brush, but I soldiered on. Between my map and my phone I was certain that I was close, but I was so focused on my guides that I must've missed the branch that slammed into my chest and knocked me back.

Stunned, I landed hard on my butt and cursed as the map and my phone both went flying. I scrambled for my phone before the screen shut off, but the map was nowhere to be seen. I rubbed the screen on my jeans to clean the dirt off and I peered at my position. I was almost there—just a few more feet. I'd make a rubbing of the tombstone, take a few pics and hightail it back to my rented car before the rain hit. I stuffed the phone in my pocket and kept both eyes peeled for the branch that had attacked me, but no further plants attempted to assault me.

I emerged into a small garden—or the remains of one. I'd become accustomed to neglected locations in my travels for the team, who seemed to delight in sending me to abandoned, crumbling sites. The grass was overgrown and invaded the stone pathway that ringed the area. Enormous rosebushes had once been penned in by said path but now sprouted in every direction. The lush red roses bloomed bright, their crimson passion almost sacrilegious in the mournful, forgotten setting. A marble angel spread her wings wide in the center of the clearing, sheltering the final resting place of Angela Rodríguez de Mendoza. Vines had grown up around the statue like living restraints, and the statue's surface was smudged with dirt that had been streaked by the recent rain. It almost looked like the angel was crying.

"Whatever you do, don't blink," I whispered.

I flinched at a crack of thunder, and it spurred me into action. I wove my way through the rosebushes toward the base of the statue. Huh. Angela had her own personal shrine. Why wasn't she with the rest of her family? The name and dates were right. I stepped closer and touched the engraved letters. I tried to forget eighteen. At first, senior year had been a blur of high school drama mixed with crushing academic pressure. My parents couldn't afford to send one of us to college, much less all of us, so I worked my ass off to earn every grant and scholarship I could. I got accepted to a Big Ten school. Everything seemed perfect, until one broken condom popped that life like a balloon.

Another rumble of thunder brought me back to the present

and urged me to action. I withdrew the tracing paper from my messenger bag and taped it over the marble slab. Dad would get a kick out of seeing the rubbing, as though I brought a piece of Spain home and included it as part of their anniversary present. A morbid piece, but still cool nonetheless.

"What are you doing?"

I yelped and the piece of charcoal flew from my hand and sailed into a rosebush. I whirled and faced the speaker, and the explanation flew out of my head as I stared at an angry Latin god. My mouth dried and I licked my lips as I tried to remember how to speak words—any words, English or Spanish.

The man stalked toward me, and I stared dumbly at the skintight black cotton T-shirt and the perfect abs silhouetted beneath it. The equally tight black jeans were also a lovely view, but my self-defense reflexes kicked in when he got too close for comfort. Hands raised and feet planted, I shifted into position for a throw, and the movement gave the stranger pause.

"I said, what are you doing?" he demanded. "How did you get here?"

Oh shit. Was he some sort of cemetery security? Was I about to be booked for trespassing? I should've checked with the office before tromping through with Sr. Ramos's friend's map.

"I walked."

"Through the—?" he asked. I considered myself to be fluent in Spanish, but I wasn't familiar with the last work. It sounded a bit like *border*. Maybe I'd crossed a property line.

"I'm sorry. I didn't see a fence. I..." My mouth gaped like a broken ventriloquist dummy as I suddenly realized that I had no idea how to translate *making a rubbing of a tombstone* into Spanish. "For my mother," I finally blurted. "A copy."

He frowned, and another clap of thunder agreed with his disapproval. The wind picked up and I shivered and wished for the cashmere sweater I'd left in my room, or one of the wool coats I'd left at home.

"Why does your mother need a copy of a stranger's tombstone?"

I straightened. "I'm not a stranger. I'm a relative."

The stranger stilled, then quirked one dark, slender brow. "Oh?"

"Yes. I'm compiling a family tree for my parents' anniversary, and—" A flash of lightning interrupted my explanation. A fat raindrop splashed my nose. I swore softly and dug into my bag for the poncho, but then the heavens opened and dumped rain so fast and furious that I could barely see Señor Tightpants's glower.

He grabbed my hand and pulled me after him. I should have protested, because being dragged away by an unknown Spaniard was not safe or smart. Unfortunately my pepper spray was at home in America thanks to the post-9-11 laws that wouldn't let me carry it on the plane, and the rain nearly drowned me when I opened my mouth to argue.

I coughed and sputtered as he led me through the dense woods. Every low-hanging branch and leaf seemed determined to smack me as I stumbled along, and my squishing shoes snagged on every root and stone. We emerged from the trees, hustled across a lawn, and then I nearly slammed into him as he stopped to open a door. We entered what appeared to be a mudroom, and I hugged my arms to my chest as my teeth chattered. I was soaked to the skin.

Señor Tightpants and I regarded each other in shared misery. "Wait here."

"Where is here?" I countered. "Who are you?"

He cocked his head. "Where are you from? Your accent is strange."

"I'm American. *Your* accent is strange. This whole country sounds like Sylvester from the Looney Tunes." In fact, the Spanish pronunciation of Barcelona sounded suspiciously like Barf-elona, evoking unpleasant thoughts of food poisoning.

"Americans do not speak Spanish."

"I hear that a lot."

"Wait here, Señora Americana."

I checked out his ass as he walked away and warmed myself with sinful thoughts. If I was about to be murdered, at least he was a sexy serial killer. The tiny room looked harmless enough. Several sets of work boots were lined up beneath a worn wooden bench, and coats hung from pegs on the wall. No whips, chains or bloody butcher's aprons. My messenger bag was waterproof and its contents were dry. I grabbed my phone and sighed at the solitary bar of signal as it flickered on and off. So much for calling for help.

My stoic savior—or captor, depending how you looked at it—reappeared barefoot, clad in new blue jeans and a white button-down shirt. He carried a stack of fluffy towels topped with a burgundy bathrobe.

"Give me your wet clothes and I will launder them."

I blinked and blurted, "Not unless you buy me dinner first." He burst into surprised laughter and smiled, a faint blush coloring his cheeks. "That came out wrong. I mean, I don't know you. You show up in a cemetery and drag me off like a caveman without so much as an introduction. It really doesn't inspire enough trust for me to strip and hand you my clothes."

He bowed his head in polite agreement. "I apologize. I forget my manners. I am Cris, and this is my home."

"You live in a cemetery?" How creepy was that?

He snorted. "No. I live near a cemetery. The house was built before the first graves were dug. You are welcome here. The storm will remain for some time, and I do not want you to take a chill. If you wish, I will bring you the telephone to contact your family and inform them of your location."

"Yes, please."

Cris set his bundle on the nearest bench and disappeared again, returning promptly with a cordless phone. I pondered who to call —not the hotel or Sr. Ramos, who were roughly three hours away in Madrid—so I called Piper instead.

"Hello?" Her voice was thick with sleepy confusion.

"Hey, it's Nati," I said, switching to English. "Sorry for the weird time, but I've been kidnapped by a hot Spanish guy who wants me to get naked and I want you to have a record of his phone number in case he murders me."

"You did what now?" Piper asked. Cris coughed and covered his smile with one hand. Oh shit. I'd made the same assumption that he had—Cris assumed Americans didn't speak Spanish, and I assumed Spaniards didn't speak English.

"I went to Angela's grave," I explained to Piper. "And it started Old Testament raining, and this guy brought me to dry land. Somewhere." I looked to Cris. "Where am I?"

"You are a guest in Mendoza Manor."

Something low in my gut warmed at his accented English—damn he sounded like Antonio Banderas, whose love scene with Selma Hayek in *Desperado* had been key to my sexual awakening.

"Did he just say Mendoza Manor?" Piper asked.

"Yeah."

"Let me talk to him," she demanded.

"Why?" I asked, suddenly suspicious.

"Because the grieving mother described in the article you sent me lived in, and I'm not kidding, 'the house of crying shadows' owned by the Mendoza family. I bet it's the same place. Ask him if there's any activity in the house related to—"

"No, Piper. Focus."

"Get naked," she advised. "Maybe it'll encourage him to let us investigate."

"Piper!"

"Right, right. Number recorded. If you don't call me back I call the cavalry. I got it. But I'm pretty sure a serial killer wouldn't let you call for help."

"Thanks. Hey, I didn't want to end up starring as the victim in one of those *Hostel* movies. And don't call the team," I warned before I hung up. I handed the phone to Cris. "Thank you."

"You are welcome. Nati? Natalie?" he guessed.

"Natividad."

"Lovely."

I blinked—most people found my name weird. Cris picked up the towels and inclined his head. "If you would come with me, I will show you to the powder room. Americans drink coffee, yes? I have an espresso maker."

"Yes." My shoes squished and squeaked with each step as I followed him.

"Then I will brew some while you change."

Cris left me in a small black-and-white bathroom. I was soaked to my skin, and my clothes peeled off in heavy, sopping-wet layers. I wrapped the mess in a towel, including my shoes, and debated what to do about my skivvies. Was it mortifying or sensible to let Señor Tightpants launder my unmentionables? I'd worn my plain cotton panties and bra, so it wasn't like he'd be touching my red-hot date-night attire.

What the hell? Yolo, right? I added my underwear to the pile, slipped on the robe and belted it tight. It didn't seem Cris's style, and was at least two sizes too big for him. A lingering antiseptic smell clung to the soft fabric, hinting at a senior citizen owner. Maybe he lived with his father or grandfather.

The worn wooden floors creaked beneath my bare feet as I followed the familiar scent of coffee to a large, sleek kitchen. My mouth watered at the combination of steel appliances, granite countertops and a hot guy making espresso. I stopped in my tracks and hugged my wet bundle to my chest as my ovaries exploded. He'd rolled up his sleeves, giving me a view of tan, toned forearms. Cris might be the most attractive man I'd ever met. He was taller than me but not by much, enough that he could lean down to kiss me but I'd match his height in a pair of high heels. His face had the sharp, finely sculpted lines of a Roman aristocrat, as though there was a marble bust of him somewhere in the house.

Cris looked up and my mental inventory expanded to include that his eyes were as dark as the espresso he brewed. Dear God.

He motioned me forward, and then traded my bundle for a tiny white cup of caffeinated bliss. While he disappeared with my laundry, I withdrew the genealogy folder from my bag. I set it on the kitchen island and sipped my drink. When Cris returned, I pointed to the family tree.

"This is how I'm related to Angela Rodríguez de Mendoza." I tapped Angela's name on the chart and explained how and why I'd learned the information.

"I see. You came to Spain to discover your roots?"

"No, I came for business. The roots were a bonus. Do you know Angela's story? Sr. Ramos found an article mentioning she had been murdered and her spirit wasn't at rest." I pulled the article in question from the folder and held it out to Cris. His brow furrowed as he took it.

"Where did he find this?"

"Library, I assume. Maybe the newspaper's archives if it's still around."

Cris grunted in reply and reluctantly returned the piece of paper. He rounded the island and fetched his own tiny mug.

"I don't believe in ghosts," I said. "But history is my obsession. I'd like to know what happened to Angela."

"She died."

"Everyone dies. Death is inevitable. It's what happens between birth and death that makes each person unique," I said matter-of-factly. I'd rehearsed that line often enough, using it on people who wondered why I wasted my life studying history. Then again most of those people who questioned my sanity were slaving away as cubicle trolls at nine-to-five jobs while I was flying around the world to beautiful, exotic locations.

Cris returned to the seat beside me. "It hardly matters now. The event is long since forgotten."

"History is important, even if it's one woman's history."

A vein twitched in his cheek, but footsteps from the hallway caught our attention. Cris cleared his throat and returned to speaking Spanish. "Diego! We have a guest."

An elderly gentleman shuffled into the room. He gaped at me from behind thick coke-bottle glasses, staring as though I'd grown a second head.

"This is Natividad Houlihan. She was visiting the cemetery when the storm arrived."

"Pleased to meet you, Diego. Thank you for letting me borrow your robe." I smiled, and he chuckled as he recovered his composure.

"You are most welcome. It looks quite well on you. It is poor weather to be visiting the cemetery. Did you lose someone close? A husband?"

Points to Diego for the sly attempt to find out if I was single—or newly widowed. I shook my head. "No. An ancestor, actually."

"She is related to Angela Rodríguez de Mendoza," Cris explained.

"Really? How extraordinary. That makes us family, then."

"Oh?"

Diego approached and peered at the documents spread atop the island. "Through marriage. Cousins-in-law, yes?" He pointed to a blank spot next to Angela's husband. "My ancestor was Don Cristóbal's younger brother."

"Really? Do you have any genealogical documents from that time period?" I asked, excited at the possibility of a new lead. "Or do you know where I might find some? Is there a local parish that the family was a part of? Or—"

"No," Cris said.

Diego patted my shoulder. "What he means to say is that many of the local historical records were lost in a fire a few decades ago. Old buildings, bad wiring."

"And that nosy Americans shouldn't meddle in things that don't concern them," Cris said.

I straightened and lifted my chin. "Tía Angela's murder was unsolved, and I find that concerning. There's no statute of limitations on murder." Or at least I assumed there wasn't—I wasn't exactly an expert on Spanish law.

"True." Diego shrugged and turned to Cris. "I was planning on going into town to run errands once the rain lets up. Perhaps I could give Natividad a lift back to her car then."

"Oh. Thank you," I said. "I hope it lets up soon. I'm supposed to catch the five o'clock train back to Madrid."

"In the meantime you must give her a tour of the house," Diego said.

Cris nodded, and there was something commanding about the gesture—an arrogant angle of his head and a stiff set to his shoulders, like a nobleman deigning to acknowledge a peasant. "Very well."

"Have you lived here long?" I asked.

Diego nodded. "Yes. It has been in my family for generations."

"And Cris is your son?" I guessed.

Diego blushed and cleared his throat. "No. He is the caretaker."

Odd. He seemed so at home in the kitchen, more like the lord of the manor instead of a servant. Considering their family resemblance and Diego's reaction, I wondered if Cris was a bastard son, or grandson. Like my parents' household, Spain was still Really Damn Catholic, and having a child out of wedlock carried all-caps SHAME. I should know.

"I will leave you to the tour then."

Diego left, and Cris gestured toward a different door. "This way, if you please, Señora Americana."

Portions of the house were older than the States had been united. Sections of the building had been damaged and rebuilt—mainly due to fires, but also to accommodate upgrades in technology. Cris seemed to know every inch of it, answering my questions with the skill of a seasoned tour guide, and I had a ton of questions. The study of history included a little bit of everything—art and architecture, language and literature, culture and cuisine—in order to understand what caused events. I interrogated him about oil paintings and tapestries, and every inch of space was covered with intriguing, expensive-looking knickknacks. Not that I was a good judge of value—I was terrible at predicting auction numbers on *Antiques Roadshow*. I'd always thought that Fabergé eggs looked like tacky souvenirs you'd pick up in a gift shop, but they were worth a fortune.

The air was stale and stuffy in most of the rooms we toured, as if the doors were seldom opened. A light layer of dust coated everything, and the motes stirred up by our movement swirled in the weak light. I'd become an expert in dust thanks to the show, because the team was forever being excited by but then debunking energy "orbs" as dust or bugs. Booming thunder rattled ancient vases atop their shelves, and the rain pounded against the windows so loudly that I wondered if it was mixed with hail. Then the electricity flickered and died, and I paused, uncertain of what to do.

"Should we take shelter somewhere?" I asked. "Like a basement?"

"No need. This storm is mostly bluster. Here, sit. There are candles in this cabinet." He patted an old loveseat upholstered with a thick gold brocade, and a cloud of dust wafted up at his touch. I stifled a sneeze and perched on the edge, afraid that my still damp hair would ruin it.

Cris returned with an honest-to-God candelabra and set it on the table between us—had he struck a match? I must have missed it while his back was turned. He lounged in an armchair and studied me in the candlelight.

"You are an investigator? Of what?" Cris asked.

"I'm a consultant to an American television network. Right now I scout locations to be featured on one of our series, but I do other things for the network, too. Mostly research."

"What sort of series?"

I squirmed but before I could parrot a benign answer, the heat in his regard kicked from simmer to boil, and I froze. I recovered after a moment and realized that my borrowed robe had caused a nip slip. Oops.

"Enjoying the view?" I blurted as I yanked the garment closed.

"Yes." Cris grinned, and my sex drive revved in response. "Though I profess I am somewhat nearsighted. You should come closer so that I may truly appreciate it." He patted his lap.

I laughed—most people would attempt a polite denial, so his honest lechery was sort of refreshing. "Is that so?"

"Indeed, and I fear I've misplaced my glasses. It's only polite that you oblige me."

I pictured a pair of black hipster glasses perched on his aquiline nose, and my nipples hardened. I clutched the robe a bit tighter and cleared my throat. "Well, despite what you might have seen online, American women don't usually flash our tits at strangers. Unless it's Mardi Gras, and beads are involved," I amended.

"Ah. I must admit that you are the first American woman I've met." He stroked his jaw, and I took a shaky breath. Dear lord, if my hormones didn't quiet down I might actually jump the man.

In theory, I was fine with jumping him. I carried condoms in my messenger bag for just such a purpose, but there was a science to casual sex. I had to be reasonably certain of my safety with my partner and my environment, and in this case I wasn't with either. Too many unknown variables, and really, there was no way that I was going to have sex with a man I met in a cemetery.

"I work for *Spirit Seekers*." I launched into the standard mission statement for the show, followed by my assurance that I didn't believe in the paranormal and preferred to focus on the historical details of the sites investigated.

Cris nodded as the air cooled between us, but he appeared intrigued, his brow furrowed. "So you are not a librarian?"

"No, I'm a historian."

"And you did not break the—?"

There was that word again. I frowned and shook my head. "I didn't see a fence, or a gate. No offense, but you could stand to do some landscaping out there. I got attacked by a tree branch."

"So you would say that there is no magic in your life?"

I blinked, agape. Had I misheard him again? Perhaps these were Catalan words, and not Spanish at all. Something in his question had been lost in translation, unless he thought I was boring.

"I suppose that depends on your definition," I said. "I have a good life. I enjoy this job, and I feel fortunate to have it."

"I see. Tell me of the most intriguing spot you have visited."

The corners of my mouth twitched. It was a command, not a question, and reminded me a bit of a job interview. *List your qualifications. Where do you see yourself in five years?*

"They're all intriguing, otherwise I wouldn't scout them in the first place. That's one of the perks of the job. Apparently ghosts don't bother haunting boring sites." I shifted my weight and searched for a balance between comfort and not ruining the upholstery. One of the drawbacks of having long, thick hair is that it would be wet for the foreseeable future. "There's something about Gettysburg, though. That's a battlefield from the American Civil War," I added. "It's so...ordinary. Green fields and trees. About fifty thousand soldiers were killed, wounded, or went missing. Fifty *thousand*. There's a gravity to the area, like..."

"As though the weight of history is pressing down upon you," Cris supplied.

I nodded, impressed. Not many people understood that. Most people visiting historical sites just took a few vacation photos and moved on, or filled out worksheets for their school field trip. They weren't affected by the story of what went on there. Me, I closed my eyes and imagined the acrid cloud of gun smoke, the sonic boom of cannon fire and the screams of the dying.

Historians were a morbid sort. Normal people didn't consider battlefield history appropriate for polite conversation. "Is there anywhere here like that here? My knowledge of Spanish history is pretty weak."

"Many places."

"Anywhere you would recommend?" I flinched at a crack of thunder. "Someplace less rainy?"

He quirked a smile. "I'm afraid the weather is beyond my control."

"Where is the most intriguing place you've visited?"

The smile faded as his expression sobered. “I don’t travel. I haven’t in a long time. Nowhere is pleasing to me.”

Ouch. Poor thing. I bet he couldn’t travel on a caretaker’s salary. It was rough to dream of being somewhere else when you had no way to get there.

The electricity flickered back to life and I cleared my throat. “I guess the storm is dying down.”

He nodded and rose. “Of course. I’m sure you must be eager to catch your train.”

I smiled politely, but at that moment catching my train wasn’t high on the list of things I wanted to do. I had a million questions about my ancestors, the house and its sexy caretaker, but sadly I was out of time.

# CHAPTER TWO

I just barely made it to the train. Back at the hotel in Madrid I showered, donned sweats and a T-shirt and tried to fix my ruined hair. A day of rain and travel had done it no favors, but I tamed it into a bun, woke my laptop and checked my email. I opened a message from my mother, expecting another Thanksgiving menu update. As the only family member who lived outside the Chicagoland area, I was also the only one exempt from bringing a dish, which was for the best because the only food I didn't burn was coffee. I scanned the text and froze at the closing paragraph.

I ran into Brian's parents at church. His mother says he is going through a divorce. Isn't that sad? You should send him a card to wish him well.

"A card?" I blurted. "What the actual fuck?"

I was pretty sure that they didn't make "congrats on your marital implosion" greeting cards. I hadn't spoken to Brian in years, and I had no desire to start now, or ever. If my mother was pondering reuniting me with Brian then she had officially hit rock bottom of her mission to find me a man. I made a note to call my brothers and recruit them to head Mama off at the pass before she decided to invite Brian and his family over for dinner while I was visiting. I didn't need a nervous breakdown on my vacation.

Cursing the room's lack of a minibar, I shook off the drama and checked in with the team. The call connected almost instantly. Eager beavers. I smiled as two Seekers squeezed into view.

"Nati! Hi! Did you take the EMF meter with you? Were there any hits?" Kenji blurted.

"The trip was fine, thank you. I'm feeling well. How are you?" I asked.

"English, Nati," John said. Kenji was excitable like a puppy, and John was the team's calm center. "How is the rain in Spain?"

I laughed and switched languages. "A lot like the rain in London. Anyway, I didn't bring the meter with, but tomorrow I'm visiting La Casa de las Siete Chimeneas. It's promising, and it has strong historical connections that the network will like."

"Take the EMF meter this time," Kenji said.

John shook his head. "Nati doesn't know how to use it."

It was a partial truth—I knew how to turn the Electromagnetic Field Detector on, and it wasn't complicated to use. I just didn't want to look like a lunatic wandering around in public with ghost-hunting equipment. Particularly during the day, when any paranoid soul might think I was up to nefarious purposes. Besides, it didn't matter what I found. The team always dug up some "evidence" of paranormal activity.

"Where's Piper?" I asked.

Kenji snorted. "She went to the kitchen to get more pickles. She'll be right back."

I nodded. Piper was the sole female member of the team. She'd started off as one of their researchers, but when the network realized she was an attractive female they talked her into becoming an investigator. Ratings jumped, unsurprisingly, but now that Piper was pregnant with her first child I doubted she'd be eager to travel. One of the producers had approached me to gauge my interest in investigating when Piper was on maternity leave. I politely told him hell no. I had zero interest in stumbling around in pitch darkness, asking for restless spirits to make their presence known.

"Why are you all in the office now?" I asked. There was a six hour time difference between Madrid and the *Seekers* team's office, so it was early there. "Aren't you all supposed to be taking time off?"

"From filming, yes, but we always have investigating to do," John said. "We've been getting nonstop calls since Halloween. All of the groups in our association are." Their team was part of an international network of paranormal investigation groups, which came in handy for finding leads on new locations.

"Because of the live show?" I asked. Crazy bastards had spent four hours investigating an abandoned insane asylum. I'd thought that place was bad during the day—mold, rusting medical equipment, bizarre acoustics that convinced you that someone was following you.

"No. Huge boost in demonic activity. One of the members of the Chicago chapter was shoved down a set of stairs. Broke his leg."

"We have their footage on our site if you want to see it," Kenji said. "Though they only had hand-helds, not sweet professional cameras like ours, so they didn't catch the entity itself."

Of course they didn't. Apparitions always appeared off camera. The guy probably tripped because he was navigating a flight of stairs in the dark by the view of a three-inch-wide screen.

"Nati!" Piper greeted me with an excited grin. Kenji vacated his chair for her and wandered off-screen. "Oh my God, girl. You hit the paranormal jackpot!"

"I did? Is that good?" I asked.

"It's awesome," Piper said. "Before it went off the grid, the House of Weeping Shadows was said to be one of the most haunted locations in Europe."

"Hence the name, I assume." I rolled my eyes. "It was a totally normal place. Kind of dusty, but normal."

"Did you take any readings?" Piper asked.

"Must have slipped my mind. What did you find out?"

"Lots." Piper grabbed her reading glasses from atop the desk and began shuffling through printouts. "I'm going to email you a PDF of everything I found. It's pretty dramatic stuff. Angela was engaged to marry the lord of the house. It was a big society deal, but she was murdered on their wedding night. Everyone thought that the husband did it, and he vanished without a trace. There's some speculation that he was killed as well, like a jealous ex did them both in and tried to frame him." Piper stopped and shrugged.

"Damn. So that's why she's supposed to be haunting the place?"

"Yup, got it in one. Spain wasn't as big in the Spiritualist movement as England was, but séances were popular for a while. As was spirit photography. Check these out." Piper held up a black-and-white photo of a spectral woman in white descending a staircase that I remembered from the tour. I frowned—photos had been easy to fake long before the invention of Photoshop. She held up another shot of a shadowy figure looming in the window of an upper floor.

"Okay. And?"

"It's an interesting location," John said. "For years it had all kinds of reported activity. Footsteps, disembodied voices, apparitions. And then the reports stopped, and there weren't any mentions after that."

"Is that normal?"

He nodded. "It's pretty standard for older locations. The activity will go dormant until something stirs it up again, like renovations or new owners."

"Fun." I stretched and rolled my shoulders. "Cris did mention that it had been renovated a few times."

"Cris?" Piper asked.

"The caretaker. He and the owner didn't mention any recent activity."

"We'd still like to pursue it," John said.

"No way. It's too pretty. No one's going to want to watch you stumble around a well-appointed luxury home."

"It would be a nice change," Piper said. "I'm still sneezing from last night's location."

"I thought you were going to take it easy?" I asked.

"I am. Just not yet." She patted her just barely showing belly. "Besides, our workload has practically tripled. We've been getting calls nonstop."

I nodded. "Yeah, John mentioned that."

"The producers would die if we could link you to a local site." Kenji popped back into view, his hands moving a mile a minute in energy-drink-inspired enthusiasm. He was the team's gadget geek, an engineer who lived on ramen noodles and Red Bull. "Not just a haunted foreign location, but one with a personal connection to the team."

I bit my tongue before replying that I wasn't one of the team—more like an independent contractor. But a special episode would mean a ratings bump, and a ratings bump would ensure that we all had jobs for another year. Plus I was saving for the dream of going back to school to get my doctorate—Natividad Houlihan, PhD, sounded like heaven to me. I'd be the first person in my family to become a doctor, even if it was an academic doctor and not a medical one.

"We'll put it on the list of potentials," I said. "I'll send you the homeowner's contact information. Maybe Legal can coax him into an agreement."

"Sweet! You're the best, Nati," Kenji said.

I chuckled. I wasn't sure about that, but if the show shot an episode there we'd have more time—and funding—to delve into Angela's story. It'd be a fabulous addition to my genealogical workup. I'd covered my father's side of the family during last season's trip to Ireland. There hadn't been any famous, infamous or royal connections—as it turned out, we came from a long line of shipbuilders and fishermen, which was hilarious considering that most of my siblings and I couldn't swim and had a history of seasickness. I survived air travel through generous doses of Dramamine.

We chatted a bit about plans for the rest of my site visits, and then I ended the call and left them to review the "evidence" from their investigation. I checked my email again and scowled at my mother's message still lurking in my inbox, and I shut down my laptop.

I shivered as the room's AC kicked on—apparently it was set for a heat wave and not a monsoon. Fat drops of rain splattered the windowpane like a Pollack painting as my forehead thumped against the glass. It was slightly more comfortable than banging my head against the desk, and the view was better.

Brian. Really? Of all the skeletons in my closet why did my mother have to dredge up that one? Desperation, most likely. My relationship with Brian was the closest I'd ever been to settled. I shuddered—my life had nearly been over at eighteen. Well, not quite as over as Angela Rodríguez de Mendoza's had been, but still...

Caretaker Cris had been right about one thing—nosy Americans shouldn't meddle in things that didn't concern them. Some things were better off forgotten.

~

I frowned at the open pieces of luggage arranged atop my bed. I was an expert at packing, but I also had myriad relatives to buy souvenirs for, and finding a place to pack everything without incurring additional baggage fees was a tricky process.

The room phone rang and interrupted my ponder, and I answered it. It was far too early to be my driver, unless something had happened. I didn't want to make alternate plans for getting to the airport.

"There is a gentleman here to see you. He says he is your cousin."

"Señor Mendoza?" Huh. Weird. Had I forgotten something in

his car? Wait, I hadn't told Cris or Diego where I was staying. How could he be here? Did the network give him the information?

Curiosity got the best of me. "Okay. Tell him I'll be right down."

I grabbed my bag and left the luggage alone for now. I had a few hours before I needed to catch my flight, and if nothing else I could cram everything into my bags and pray that it survived the trip.

I stepped into the spacious, sunlit lobby and spotted Diego waiting for me near the reception desk. I smiled and shook his hand—he looked charming in his tweed jacket and pleated pants, like an emeritus professor visiting for a lecture.

"Good afternoon, cousin Natividad."

"It's lovely to see you again, cousin Diego. To what do I owe this visit?"

"It is a bit difficult to explain. May we speak in the café?" He looked sheepish, fiddling with the handle of a leather attaché case. Diego's wiry white eyebrows reminded me of my grandfather, who had wild brows that always gave him a slightly cartoonish look.

"Of course."

He ordered a cup of tea and I ordered coffee, because a dose of caffeine might help my packing decisions. "What's on your mind?"

"I have spoken with your television network about using the manor as a location for a future episode, and I would like to offer the opportunity for you to investigate the estate. You would be the first investigator to do so since 1897."

"Thank you. That's wonderful." I could almost hear the team squealing in joy across the Atlantic.

"There are conditions, and they are...unconventional."

"Oh?" That sounded ominous.

Diego nodded and produced a contract from his case. Kudos to the man for coming prepared. Few people understood the need for insurance and the other million legal details necessary for filming on location. He slid the paperwork toward me across the table—one copy in English and one in Spanish.

"Before I will allow your team to investigate, you must stay in the manor alone for a fortnight."

I blinked. "Me? But I'm not an investigator. I'm the location scout. I don't even believe in ghosts."

"I understand—"

"And I'm leaving today. In a few hours, in fact." I checked my watch, just to be sure.

"Your flight can be rescheduled, yes?"

"Well...yes. But Thanksgiving is next week. I'm going home to spend the holiday with my family." Though I didn't really *need* to go home for Thanksgiving, because I was also going home for Christmas and New Year's. And I didn't have any time-sensitive assignments at the moment. I wasn't due to scout the next international location until next month, and the next few weeks were supposed to be devoted to research, most of which I could do anywhere with internet access. Hypothetically, I could stay and do this.

I sipped my coffee. What the hell would I do alone for two weeks in a Spanish manor? Maybe I could start writing a novel, or a collection of short stories like a proper American abroad. Or have loads of hot sex with the caretaker...

"Wait, alone? You and Cris won't be there?" I asked.

"No. I will be in a treatment center. I have cancer," he admitted.

"Oh, I'm so sorry." I squeezed his hand in sympathy, and he patted my hand amiably.

"Thank you. It was hard when I was first diagnosed, but I am coming to terms with it. Cris will be on the grounds during the day, but he leaves at nightfall. He does not know about this offer. I thought it best to hear your answer first."

"Our legal team will need to review the contract before I can commit to anything."

"Of course. I will be leaving Tuesday afternoon, so please let me know your answer before then."

I nodded. My coffee was too hot and too strong, but I didn't trust myself not to blurt anything inappropriate while my mind whirled with possibilities. The chance to be the first investigators in a haunted location in over one hundred years was something that the network would eat up. Great ratings bump potential.

"Why me?" I asked. "Why do you want me to stay there?"

Diego nodded. "That is a fair question. It is because of your tie to Angela. I hope that your presence may finally allow her spirit to rest. The estate will have new owners after I pass, and they may not respect her as family would. This may be her only opportunity to find peace."

I resisted the urge to state again that I don't believe in ghosts, but it was a lovely sentiment. "So the house is still haunted?"

"All old homes are haunted to some degree or another. The walls hold secrets like a sponge, drawing in heartache and holding on to it for years to come. Why do you work with believers when you do not believe?"

"Because I get to travel to beautiful cities and see amazing things." I smiled and shrugged. "Though I also travel to abandoned insane asylums and old battlegrounds. I like this trip much better."

"Good. I look forward to hearing your answer."

Diego left, and I chugged the rest of the coffee. It burned a scorching path down my throat and settled in an acidic puddle in my stomach that sloshed around as I hurried back to my room. It would be late where the team was—or early, depending how you looked at it—but I knew some of them would be in the office. Paranormal investigators were creatures of the night, like vampires. I called the office on my cell first and got Kenji.

"I have news. Who else is there?"

"Just me and John doing evidence review. Why?"

"Because I have news. Skype me."

"Now? I thought you were leaving?"

"Apparently not. Skype. Now."

"All right."

Kenji and John popped into view when the call connected. I

explained the situation, and their eyes widened like surprised anime characters as I spoke.

"Whoa," Kenji said when I finished. "This is epic. Seriously epic. You have to do this."

"I don't *have* to do anything," I corrected. "This doesn't seem weird to you guys? Wait, forget I asked that." Nothing seemed weird to them, because they were the weird ones. "I'm going to scan this agreement, send it to Legal and let them draw up a counter. If I'm agreeing to this—and it's still an *if*—then I want to make sure we're not liable for damages or anything."

"I'll call the British chapter," John said. "They can loan you equipment."

"No." I held up my hands as though trying to stop a runaway bull from trampling me. "No equipment. I'm not investigating."

Kenji scowled. "Nati, you can't spend two weeks in a haunted house without investigating. That's sacrilege."

"Sure I can."

"What are you going to do for two weeks then? Read books and work on your tan?" he countered. I stuck my tongue out at him, and John chuckled.

"We'll set up a wireless hotspot so we can walk you through investigating. It'll be painless."

Yeah, right. Because having the entire team watching my every move while I stumbled around in the dark was going to be simple. I inhaled a deep, calming breath. "I'm supposed to be there alone."

"You'll be alone. Can you extend your stay at the hotel for two more days?"

"I think so." They didn't seem to be fully booked at the moment. Canceling my flight was going to be a pain in the ass, and Homeland Security was going to give me some serious side-eye when I got home. They got cranky about people changing their plans, especially people of color, as if being brown skinned and dark haired meant I was more susceptible to converting to Islam and taking up jihad.

John nodded. "Okay. Send the paperwork. We'll take care of stuff on our end while you work on your flight and hotel."

"Okay, but I'm not agreeing to anything until Legal gives the all clear, so keep me updated."

I ended the call and sighed. I wanted to believe that I'd just set myself up for a two-week paid vacation, and imagined politely asking Cris to rub suntan oil on my back. And my front... Clearing my throat, I picked up the room phone and called the front desk.

I spent a cranky hour and a half arguing with the airline in English and in Spanish until my flight was changed, cancelling today's flight in exchange for a voucher for my return flight. It helped that I was a platinum member with a buttload of frequent flyer miles, so they were inclined to keep my business. The hotel was happy to have me for an additional stay. I moved my luggage from the bed to the floor and stretched out for a nap until my cell rang, displaying the name of one of the legal department's interns. I guess the bigwigs didn't get out of bed for D-list shows like mine.

"Hello, Jane. How are you?"

"Do you have any idea what time it is here?"

"Coffee o'clock?" I guessed. Jane snorted, so at least I was funny.

"Pretty much. The good news is that there's nothing hidden in the paperwork."

"And the bad news?" I asked.

"It's not really bad news, just more news. You're not contracted for work like this. I'm sending an amendment to your contract that will allow you to be covered under the network's insurance for the length of your stay."

I chewed my bottom lip. "I sense a 'but' attached to that statement."

"But it opens you up to more work like this. They might want you to become an investigator. Especially with Piper being away on maternity leave. They need another woman on the team."

Damn it. I swallowed a groan and forced a strained "okay."

"It means more money, though."

"How much more money?" I asked, curious.

Jane listed a number, and my eyebrows rose. Hot damn. I could put a down payment on a condo for that. *Equity.* My mouth watered at the idea of my very own piece of real estate—a permanent home base. I could move my books out of storage and into my very own research library. Surely that was worth the embarrassment of a little ghost hunting. Or, better yet, I could save it for tuition. *Today's lecture is being presented by Dr. Natividad Houlihan...*

"Done. Let's get everything signed, sealed and delivered."

## CHAPTER THREE

I peered out of the window as the taxi approached the house, taking the time to study it that I'd missed during my previous mad dash through the storm. The structure was strong and intimidating like a fortress, but it was beautiful. Stately. The sky was still a brooding shade of gray thanks to the lingering rain, and it added a melancholy air to the place. The house—mansion really—was built from a light gray stone and accented with curling wrought iron and carved stonework details. The surrounding trees added softness to the estate. Or menace, depending how you looked at it. Brooding Spanish trees, hiding God knew what.

I wasn't sure how I'd do with only trees and the internet for company for two weeks. And Cris... My pulse accelerated as the taxi slowed to a stop. I hadn't had a roommate in years, and definitely never a sexy roommate with sculpted cheekbones and smoldering eyes that were as dark as a triple espresso.

I stepped out slowly so I didn't slip on the damp gravel driveway. I'd had to request a minivan from the taxi company in order to schlep all the ghost-hunting gear in addition to my overstuffed luggage. I needed to do laundry. Did that make me a bad guest? "Hi. Glad to be here. Where's your utility room?"

The front door creaked open. Damn. It was massive, almost a drawbridge, and made of heavy, dark wood. Oak maybe? Did they have oaks in Spain?

Diego stepped out. His face seemed thinner somehow, even though it had barely been two days since I'd seen him last. He wheeled a small black suitcase behind him, and I felt terribly overpacked.

"Is that all you're taking?" I blurted. Real smooth, Nati.

Diego chuckled. "I don't need much in the hospital. Pajamas and slippers, they said."

"Are you... Will you be all right?" I swallowed hard. I'd lost two grandparents and a great-aunt to cancer. It was nasty business, and a long, hard way to die.

Diego glanced at the taxi driver unloading my stuff, then stepped closer. "No. It is terminal. The doctors, they say they can get me more time, and perhaps ease the pain."

"Oh. I'm so sorry."

"Everyone dies." He paused and glanced back at the house, then smiled sadly. "The only thing we can do is live as best we can before it happens."

Diego asked the taxi driver to place everything in the foyer and promised a healthy tip for his effort (which I'd been planning on anyway, because the poor bastard had to lug all those equipment cases). I followed Diego inside.

"I hate to ask this, but can you tell me—" I stopped and swallowed, my face burning with an embarrassed blush. "Can you tell me where the hot spots of paranormal activity are in the house? I have to know, for the team. They harassed me about it."

He chuckled again. "Of course. First, I will let you know, Cris comes and goes during the day but he leaves at sundown. You may see little of him, because he is sulking."

I swallowed the reply that I hoped to see plenty of Cris. "Sulking?"

Diego nodded. "He abhors the thought of your American investigators invading the house and tracking mud over the floors."

"Ah, right. Doesn't Cris being here violate the agreement? I'm not technically alone in the house though if he's present."

"No. Cris is the caretaker. He is as much a part of the house as the walls."

I frowned, because the treating-servants-as-furniture thing was much too privileged for me.

Our first stop was the guest room I'd be staying in, which was a baroque fantasy including an enormous four-poster bed with actual bed curtains. I wanted to jump on it just to see if the mattress had real old-timey springs. The room was cool and damp, and it smelled of lemon furniture polish and floral potpourri. Very old lady, but kind of charming. There was an honest-to-goodness dressing table with an oval mirror. It ought to have crystal perfume bottles atop it and little feminine odds and ends, but it was sadly bare. I could fix that. I really wanted to sit and comb my hair like a movie star in a period piece.

"This was to be Doña Angela's room," Diego said. "She married Cristóbal Mendoza Ríos, who was head of the household at the time. She was found here in this room on her wedding night, stabbed to death."

I shuddered, the homey aura fading as I thought of the poor woman dying in this very spot. Then I took a deep breath and squared my shoulders. It was tragic but hardly extraordinary. Europe was covered with millennia of death and murder. The States probably were too, but our recorded history only went back a few centuries because it started with the invasion of Europeans. I hated the idea of lost history—an entire swath of our human heritage was missing thanks to assholes distributing smallpox-riddled blankets. The native Mexican branches of my mother's family tree weren't documented until Christianity appeared to baptize them.

"Did they catch her killer?" I asked.

"No. Many thought it was Don Cristóbal, because he disappeared the same day. Our family believes that he was killed as well, both deaths at the hand of his jealous former lover."

Men were such dogs. He must have epically failed that breakup to turn his lover homicidal. "What kind of ghostly activity happens here?"

"There have been reports of a woman weeping, and an apparition of a woman in white."

I nodded. Pretty standard. The team would like it. Though that also meant they'd want to put a camera in my bedroom. Not happening.

"Anything else?" I asked.

Diego hesitated, and I quirked a brow. "Well," he began, "there is a story of a medium who slept in this room going mad. She was the last spiritualist to investigate the manor. Since then we have kept our guests to the mundane variety, and no one has reported any experiences."

A chill shivered down my spine and I swallowed hard—I'd scouted enough abandoned insane asylums to guess how the poor medium ended up. How terrified did you have to be to go insane? It seemed unlikely—really, how scary could one weeping woman be?

"When was this?" I asked.

"1897."

"Ah. It really didn't take much to drive a woman mad in the nineteenth century. I'd lose my mind if I was expected to stay at home all day and look after the house." The Victorians had even invented the vibrator as a method to relieve hysteria—an innovation that generations of women, and men, had been grateful for.

"You do not wish to be married?"

"My definition of married involves seeing the world with my husband, not being confined by four walls covered in yellow wallpaper." I waved a hand and dismissed further comment, because I'm sure the literary reference didn't translate. "What's next?"

We moved from room to room, and I recorded notes of the many incidences of paranormal activity—disembodied footsteps, strange growls, shadowy figures, same old, same old. I was glad that there wasn't a creepy attic, but there was definitely a dungeony cellar that the team was going to insist that I crawl around in. I hoped there was bug spray somewhere in the manor, because I wasn't going down there without a way to mass murder some spiders. I wasn't afraid of ghosts, but spiders terrified me.

The cab driver waited in the foyer next to my mountain of gadgets, and I paid the driver and bid Diego goodbye.

Diego clasped my hand and smiled sadly. "Good luck, cousin. I hope you have a pleasant stay."

I smiled. "So do I. I wish you had a swimming pool, though."

He laughed. "Perhaps the next owner will put one in."

Diego left, and the enormous wooden door shut behind him. A pang of sadness tightened my chest. It seemed a shame that the home would pass to a stranger after generations of Diego's family had lived there. So many things would die with him, a legacy of stories and hand-me-down heirlooms that wouldn't matter to anyone but a relative.

I sighed because my inner history major was showing, and then focused on unpacking my luggage. Thankfully the manor had plenty of modern amenities. The only thing missing was a computer with high speed internet, but I'd brought my own computers and a Wi-Fi hub. It was pretty neat, and it was by far the only piece of technology I was really interested in using. No idea how it worked, but I plugged it in and poof! Secure wireless internet! The range wasn't so hot, though, and probably wouldn't reach the cellar. Maybe I could use that as an excuse not to investigate it.

I unpacked, threw a load of laundry into the washer (which was far nicer than the unit in my apartment building), and Skyped the team. I picked the dining hall to set up the command center in—I couldn't help but roll my eyes at even thinking the term. I dreaded pretending to be an investigator.

"Did you take any readings?" Kenji asked.

"No. I started a load of laundry."

Piper giggled in the background, and John shouldered Kenji

out of the way. "Give us the tour, and we'll decide where to set up the cameras."

I nodded, swapped the camera on my tablet to face out and then started a walkthrough of the house. I recited the notes I'd taken as I went, and the team muttered comments about cameras, EVP sessions and other paranormal technobabble.

"What activity happens in the kitchen?"

"None," I replied. "But the entrance to the cellar is here. It's used as a wine cellar, and there are no experiences reported there. That means I don't have to investigate it, right?"

"Wrong. We always investigate the cellar," John said.

"But there are spiders down there. Spanish spiders. They probably drink sangria and dance flamenco."

"Speaking of which, where's the sexy Spanish guy?" Piper asked.

"No idea. Haven't seen him yet today. Diego said he's off somewhere pouting because I'm scuffing the floors with my filthy American shoes." I turned to head to the next location and ran smack into Cris's chest. I yelped and dropped my tablet—thank God I'd shelled out for the expensive shatterproof case, otherwise the screen would've cracked when it bounced across the tile floor and slid under the fridge.

I swore and dove after it, the muted voices of my team calling out to ask if I was all right (and if I was taking readings).

"I'm fine. It's just Cris. And I dropped you. Literally." My fingers combed through dust bunnies and crumbs until I brushed the edge of the tablet and pulled it free. "I'll call you back."

"Wait, I want to see how hot he is—" Piper protested as I cut the call.

I sat back on my heels and looked up at Cris, who studied me with a bemused expression.

"What are you doing?" he asked.

"A walkthrough of the house. For the team I work for. Well, with. I work for the network. Don't you make any noise when you walk?"

He glanced down, and I blushed at the sight of his bare feet.

Cris wiggled his toes for emphasis, and lustful heat bizarrely coiled in my belly. I didn't have a foot fetish, but for some reason it seemed naughty that his bare feet were right next to me. The perverse urge to caress an ankle increased my blush from sunburn to second degree burn.

I cleared my throat primly. "What happened to your shoes?"

"My shoes were muddy from the garden, where I was working, not pouting. I took them off."

I shifted to rise, and he held out a hand to help me. I took it, and the lustful heat in my belly kicked from simmer to boil. "You could've been multitasking. Working and pouting at the same time."

Cris frowned. "I do not pout."

"There's no way you were born with those lips and have never pouted." The observation rolled off my tongue before my brain warned my mouth that it was impolite to voice that opinion.

The corners of his mouth twitched. "Perhaps. I disapprove of Diego's decision. I do not like the idea of a private home being broadcast to the world for some ridiculous ghost hunt."

"If it makes you feel any better, I agree. Or at least I agree about the ghost part. I disagree about broadcasting."

"Oh?"

"Paranormal investigation makes up about half of our air time. The rest is spent on the history of the area and how it ties into the investigation. We hook viewers with the spirits, and they don't even realize that they are learning history. It's pretty clever."

Cris tilted his head as he regarded my tablet. "This is the most recent model?"

"For now. I think they're releasing a new one in the first quarter next year."

"I don't doubt it. Every time I purchase a gadget it becomes obsolete just when I become accustomed to it, or it breaks. The hard drive on my laptop became corrupted and I have not purchased a new one yet. May I?"

I handed him the tablet and stepped close to show him a few

of the upgraded features. Roses—Cris smelled of roses. I bet the garden was as beautiful.

"I need to call the team back," I said. "Would you like to meet them?"

He nodded, and I reconnected the call. "Hi, guys. This is Cris, the caretaker. He speaks English." *So please don't say anything stupid or embarrassing.*

The team introduced themselves one by one, and Cris nodded politely. "You hunt ghosts for a living?" he asked when they finished.

"We do when we're filming," John said. "We all have day jobs between seasons."

"Even you?" Cris asked me.

"No, I'm employed by the network. I consult for other shows as well."

"She has an office and everything," Kenji said.

"I'm going to continue the tour. Would you like to come with me?" I asked Cris. "Any information you have would be helpful."

He chuckled. "I am a skeptic, like you. I don't know anything about ghosts."

"Do you think the manor is haunted?" John asked him.

"Haunted? No. Much of the building is quite old. The floors creak and the pipes bang. It can be disturbing to a superstitious mind."

"Good thing I have a reasonable mind then," I joked.

"I will leave you to your tour. I have a few things to attend to before nightfall." Cris waved goodbye to the team, and I admired the view as he walked away.

"Is he gone?" Piper asked.

"Yup."

"Damn, girl. I wish I could spend two weeks with that."

"Hey," Kenji said. He sounded defensive, but his hurt feelings were only for show. Kenji was deep in the closet due to his disapproving family, and he always made a point of flirting on camera.

I'd met his boyfriend once and they were super adorable together, like hyper, geeky puppies.

"Focus, people," I said. "If you want me to investigate tonight then I'm going to need to start setting up."

We finished the tour, and then I began the arduous process of setting up the cameras throughout the house. Unlike a typical investigation, these cameras would be up and running for the length of my stay, and the team would be monitor them live as well as review footage for EVPs and other anomalies. I was a little paranoid at the idea of being constantly filmed, but the team assured me that it was an awesome idea.

I fidgeted with camera angles under the team's supervision —"No, up a little. Wait, now left. No, that's still not right."—and ran cable from each camera to the "command center" dining room. Kenji instructed me in the finer points of taping down cords so I wouldn't trip over them in the dark and break my neck. Just before dinnertime I had everything up and connected, and I ended the call in order to find something to eat before my first ghost-hunting adventure. I found Cris puttering around in the kitchen.

"I am leaving shortly. Is there anything you need before I go?" he asked.

*Yes. Take your shirt off.* "No, not that I can think of."

"Very well. I will see you tomorrow. Good luck with your investigation." He smiled dryly, and we shared a skeptical laugh.

"Thanks."

With the headset on I felt like a call center employee about to survey dearly departed customers, but it let me talk to the team and kept my hands free to operate gadgets (of which there were many). An EMF detector, motion detectors, a laser grid generator, a digital thermometer to detect cold spots, a digital voice recorder for EVP sessions. The S3, a Spirit Speak & Say that allowed spirits to communicate through it like E.T. phoning home. I was a little fuzzy on the science behind how that one worked, because it was one of their more controversial pieces of equipment, as was the Spirit Scanner, which rapidly scanned audio frequencies in search of real-time EVPs. The thing was loud as hell and had a habit of also picking up radio stations and baby monitors, but the team loved it.

"Are you ready to go lights out?" John asked.

"As ready as I'll ever be." I scowled as I adjusted my headset.

"You'll be fine," he assured me. I insisted on John as my main contact, because he was the most level-headed. The others argued in the background like the barking of excited puppies. "Let's start with the cellar."

"No!"

"Just kidding."

"Not funny," I muttered. "You know I have poor night vision, right?"

It was a side effect of urban living. It was never truly dark in the city, not even when the power went out. The first time I'd spent a night outside Chicago, during a family vacation to the Wisconsin Dells, I was shocked by the darkness of the sky and the brightness of the stars.

"You'll adjust. Use the screen on the handcam to guide you when you move around."

"This little screen? It's like two inches wide."

Kenji called out "That's what she said!" in the background. I swallowed the urge to tell him to go fuck himself. No f-bombs allowed on our network.

"You'll be fine," John assured me in a soothing tone of voice.

"Are you afraid of the dark?" Kenji teased.

"Yes," I snapped. "Do you know how many people are murdered, mugged, or assaulted after sundown? I do, because there are cops in my family. The dark is fu—frickin' terrifying."

"Nothing is going to assault you," John said.

"There could be spiders," I said. A sigh hissed through the headset. "Or mice."

"You're perfectly safe, Nati. Let's start on the second floor where the footsteps are reported. Bring the geophones with you."

Geophones are little black plastic cylinders about the size of soda cans that emit flashing lights and irritating beeps when vibration is detected. Supposedly they would trigger if ghostly footsteps walked past them. If the footsteps were the product of the house settling, wouldn't that cause vibrations to set them off? Or banging plumbing in the walls or beneath the floor?

I turned lights off throughout the house, and then under John's direction I placed four geophones along the hallway outside of the family bedrooms. Diego had given us permission to investigate his room, but I insisted on respecting his privacy while he was gone. Besides, there were no reports to investigate in there anyway.

I turned off the final set of lights and plunged the hallway into darkness. My pulse raced, the beat impossibly loud in my ears as I exhaled a shaky breath. I wasn't just scared of the dark, I hated it. I always slept with a light on somewhere, like the kitchen or bathroom. Darkness was an opportunity for my younger siblings to leap out of hiding and scare the shit of me.

"Okay. Now what?" I asked.

"We want to do an EVP session in your room to contact the spirit of Angela."

I rolled my eyes. "Right."

I refused to set up one of the constantly running cameras in my bedroom, so I brought my tablet with me up to the room along with a handcam. I set them on the dressing table and then stood next to the bed, feeling like an idiot as I switched the voice recorder on. I wiped my sweating palms on the seat of my jeans.

"What do I say?"

"Ask questions," John explained. "Like if she has anything to tell us, or if she knows how she died. Be polite. Spirits who were victimized don't take well to being provoked so it's best to treat them with respect."

"In English or Spanish?"

"Use both. It'll make the network happy. Make sure you mark

the spot if you bump into anything, or cough or shuffle your feet. Makes it easier for the team to ignore it."

Or tripped, fell and busted something in the dark. Alone. How far was I from the nearest emergency room? I was definitely asking Cris about that in the morning. If I broke my damn neck wandering around in the dark, there'd be two spirits haunting this room.

"All right. Here goes nothing." I rolled my shoulders, took a deep breath and turned off the bedside lamp.

I started the EVP session by introducing myself and explaining my distant familial tie to Angela. Then I started with the questions. John quietly prompted me, instructing me to add pauses between each question to allow the spirit time to answer. The silence unnerved me. I had always lived in a city—first Chicago, and now the dubious civilization of Chevy Chase, Maryland—and there was always ambient noise. Humming car engines, the drone of passing jet planes, the shuffle of feet on concrete sidewalks, barking neighborhood dogs, and so on and so forth. But the manor was surrounded by stoic Spanish trees that insulated it from the noise of Barcelona below. As I strained to catch phantom answers to my interview, all I heard was the sound of my breath and the murmur of the team over the headset.

Then I jumped as I walked into a cold spot near the wardrobe.

"Whoa."

"Whoa what?" John asked.

"It's freezing right here." I reached with my free hand and shivered as goose bumps marched up my arm. I felt for the edges of the spot to figure out what was causing it. Air conditioning was my first assumption, but the manor didn't have AC. The windows were shut, but it could still be a draft—they weren't exactly weather-tight, energy-efficient windows. I aimed the digital thermometer at the spot, and it read as fifteen degrees cooler than the rest of the room.

"Ask questions," John prompted. "And do you smell anything? Perfume? Flowers?"

I frowned—I was supposed to ask a cold spot questions? Right... I sniffed the air. "Just my coconut body wash."

John sighed. "You need unscented products for an investigation to avoid contamination."

"Well, I didn't pack for an investigation. Shush. Is that you, Angela? Are you making this room colder?"

"Ask her to lower the temperature further."

"Can you please lower the temperature another five degrees?" I stared at the readout as degrees ticked down one by one until it reached the temperature I asked for.

Holy shit.

I whacked the thermometer against my thigh. I set the camera down and used the light from the screen to yank the batteries out and check them. Double As. I was sure I had some in my travel bag.

Ignoring John's questions I pulled the headset off and set it on the bed as I changed the batteries in the thermometer. When I returned to the place where I'd encountered the cold spot it was gone, and the temperature matched the rest of the room. For good measure I walked around and looked for it, but everything read normal.

I pulled the headset back on to the sound of John lecturing me for taking it off. "Okay. Debunked. What next?"

"Next time keep your headset on. And we're making a note to check all of the batteries tomorrow. We usually do before each investigation, but this is unique."

"Ooh, I feel special," I joked. Someone snickered.

"The geophones are triggering. Go back to the command center and get the thermal camera."

Right. I brought the pile of gadgets back to the dining room and picked up the thermal camera. It was a neat toy that made me want to quote Arnold Schwarzenegger lines from *Predator*. As the name implied, the camera showed heat signatures. I waved my hand in front of the lens, resulting in a psychedelic display on the screen.

"Groovy," I said.

John chuckled. "If there are heating elements under the floor or critters causing the geophones to trigger, they'll show up on thermal."

"Critters?" I shuddered. I'd rather deal with ghosts than vermin.

"Yeah. You'll be fine."

The Technicolor thermal display was larger but harder to navigate by, so it was a slow journey to the geophones, and by the time I reached them they had stopped triggering. I panned up and down the silent hallway but saw nothing. With a shrug I made a slow circuit, checking the walls and ceiling. Nothing. The geophones emitted irritating high-pitched electronic squeals as I passed them.

"Maybe a truck drove by?" I guessed.

"You're too far from the road."

"Small earthquake?"

"So small that you didn't notice it in the other room?" John countered. Good point. "Try an EVP session."

"Maybe their batteries are dying, too."

"Battery drain is a sign of spirit activity," Kenji spoke up.

"Okay. I'll switch out the batteries." Only thirteen more nights of this to go. Joy.

Because I nixed having a camera in my room we settled on me keeping a handcam, a digital voice recorder and an EMF meter beside my bed so I could have them handy to document anything I experienced. Considering that it was now four in the morning the only thing I intended to experience was sleep. I donned my pajamas and went through my bedtime routine, and indulged in pampering my hair at the dressing table. I felt glamourous instead of frazzled, and I longed for some skin cream to indulge in, or an expensive lady's scent.

Exhausted, I crawled into the enormous bed and sighed happily at the luxury of high-thread-count sheets. I drifted asleep almost instantly.

The dream crept up on me stealthily, as though in stocking feet. I was in the half in, half out phase of sleep, too drowsy to care what was going on around me but aware enough to know that I was dreaming. I'd tossed and turned a bit until I was hugging a lump of covers with one bare leg draped over it. A warm, strong hand caressed my calf and slid up to rest on my upper thigh. I glanced down to make sure that I was still alone, and no one was there.

*Ooh, a sex dream.* Awesome. I'd been blessed with an exceptionally vivid imagination, but I hadn't had a good sex dream in a while. I deserved a reward after the foolishness I'd put up with all night. The last sex dream I'd had featured me peeling Idris Elba out of his skintight jaeger suit in *Pacific Rim*. Certainly memorable, but this dream called for the current object of my desire, Cris. I imagined the scent of roses that had clung to him earlier in the kitchen. I licked my lips as I visualized kissing along the line of his jaw, the neatly trimmed beard coarse beneath my lips and tongue.

I rolled onto my back and tugged off my pajama bottoms and panties, then tossed them to the floor, followed by my pajama top. I teased the nipple of one breast, rolling the bud between my fingers until it peaked. My other hand dipped between my legs to stroke my sex. My hips rose to meet my dream lover, and his cock thrust deep within me.

I teased my clit fast and hard, bringing myself to a quick climax that burst through me like a firecracker. I moaned and begged for more, because I wanted an entire fireworks display. Cris tugged my legs farther apart and gripped my knees, pushing them back so I was spread wide beneath him. His cock was hot and hard as he pumped into me, slamming all the way to the hilt before nearly withdrawing completely.

*Yes.* God, yes. I pinched my nipple hard and my back arched as ragged pleasure consumed me and left me limp and panting. For a moment I thought the dream was over, but then Cris's lips skimmed my belly. I moaned and reached for him, stroking his hair and drawing him up for a scorching kiss—almost literally. His mouth burned against mine as though he was running a high fever. It seemed an odd detail and it stuck in my sleep-addled mind, but then I dismissed it as just dream weirdness. Hey, better a hot lover than a cold fish.

Cris's lean body pressed against mine and pushed me into the mattress. He hesitated as though waiting for me to make the next move, so I wrapped myself around him and drew him close. Heavy heat enveloped me, and I cupped his ass to pull his cock deeper within me.

"More," I murmured. "Harder."

He answered with a masculine growl and a thrust of his hips. His hot mouth branded my lips, cheek and throat with kisses, his teeth nipping sharply at my earlobe as he ground out whispered demands. Dear God, dirty talk was better in Spanish. Cris listed all the ways he wanted to take me, possess me, to make me scream and beg. I replied with all the deliciously naughty things I wanted him to do during our waking hours—to bend me over the desk in the library, and to fuck me on my hands and knees on the kitchen floor. With a groan of ecstasy he came inside me, his cock pulsing as he filled me.

"Mine," Cris growled against my lips. He covered my body with rough kisses as though marking his territory.

"Yes, yours," I whispered in reply. Sated, I drifted into deep, blissful sleep.

# CHAPTER FOUR

I woke with a grin like the cat that ate the canary, still boneless and languid from fantastic dream sex. I was naked beneath the covers—so glad I refused to have a live camera in my room. The team did not need to see me masturbate, no matter how great a ratings bump we'd get from footage of my performance being leaked online. And boy, I did a number on myself during the night, judging by a few enthusiastic bruises I discovered. It wasn't the first time. I treated self-pleasure like I did any other job—if I was going to do it, then I was going to do it right—and because I liked things passionate (not necessarily rough, because I wasn't into pain per se), that meant grabbing, pinching and bruising.

I showered, dressed and braided my hair, then headed to the kitchen to brew some coffee. I nearly stumbled into Cris making tea, and I blushed so hot I was sure that steam was rising from my still-damp hair.

"Good morning!" I said, a bit too brightly.

"Good morning, Natividad. Did you sleep well?"

"Oh, yes. Very well, thank you. Did you?"

The corners of his mouth twitched as though he fought a smile. "Yes. Quite well. I had pleasant dreams."

I fumbled with the container of coffee and nearly dropped it. Thankfully it was still sealed and didn't shower everything in coffee grounds. Whew.

"Good," I said. "What are your plans today?"

"I'm securing the fountain for the winter, and a few other details. Why?"

"Would you show me the grounds later? I'd like to see the garden."

"Of course."

"I have to sit through evidence review first. Do you want to join me?"

"I'll pass."

Cris fixed Spanish tortillas, and we argued amiably over the name. I insisted that he was mistaken, for the dish he prepared was clearly an omelet with potatoes involved and not a tortilla. He informed me that the New World was mistaken and this was a true tortilla, and the discussion culminated in him silencing me with an offered bite. It was delicious, and I nearly swooned—a Latin god who could cook? He had to be too good to be true.

We ate in contented silence, because the kitchen was being covered by one of the cameras and neither of us wanted to talk with our mouths full. The team was watching us eat breakfast. Weirdos. I felt like I was living in a fishbowl, with the team staring in to see if the ghosts of goldfish past swam by.

After the dishes were done I headed to the command center and fired up Skype on the monitor. "Well?"

Kenji and John were manning the fort. "We got a few interesting footsteps, an EVP, and one anomaly."

I was not impressed, but I feigned interest. "All right. Show me what you've got."

Most of the footsteps sounded like the normal bumps and bangs one would expect from an old building settling during the night. The EVP was supposed to be a woman weeping during my interview with Angela's spirit, particularly when the cold spot appeared. I wasn't sold on that one either. It was faint and distant and could be a bird or a feral cat, or even just sound distortion.

"What's the anomaly?" I asked.

"That one's pretty cool." Kenji brought up a video file and I clicked on it. The dark footage was fast and almost impossible to see, but I spotted a shadow pass by at the end of a hallway, as though headed for the kitchen for a snack.

"Huh. Okay."

"Okay?" Kenji repeated. He placed a hand over his heart as though wounded. "How is that just okay? It's a full-bodied shadow person."

"Shadow person?" I repeated, quirking a brow. Looked like a blob to me. It could be a passing moth for all we knew.

"Yeah. They're a particular kind of haunting, usually demonic in nature. They're fast and damn hard to catch. This is great!"

*The house of weeping shadows...* I shivered but sternly reminded myself of the Latin flair for overdramatic names, as myself and my sisters Concepción, Rosario, and Magdalena could attest to.

"Uh-huh. Well, I'm going to go for a walk. You guys make a list of what you want me to investigate tonight. Not the cellar."

"You're going to have to go in there eventually."

"Later, not sooner. Bye, guys."

I retreated outside to a beautiful day. I grinned and turned my face up to the sun, soaking up the warm rays. As a Midwestern girl who'd been transplanted to the East Coast, I was used to gloomy, gray days in November, so the past few days of dealing with the rain in Spain hadn't dampened my spirits too much.

The hem of my long skirt brushed the damp grass as I wandered away from the house. I'd dressed in a colorful broomstick-style skirt and a long-sleeved blouse. Not my usual attire, because I picked the skirt with the wistful thought of Cris lifting it and discovering the cute, black lace boy short panties beneath it. I stumbled as I failed to pay adequate attention to the uneven lawn. Damn it. I needed to stop objectifying Cris. He was a person, not a character in a spicy romance novel.

Then I spotted him shirtless in the rose garden, and the voice of reason was replaced with one that exclaimed, *¡Ay, papi*!

His sweat-slicked skin glistened—honest-to-God glistened—in the warm afternoon sunlight. I licked my lips and imagined the hint of salt if I ran my tongue over the well-defined ridge of his abs. Cris turned at my approach and smiled, causing my stomach to somersault. Then he held out a rose from the bush he was pruning for the winter, and I almost swooned.

"Wow. Are you for real?" I blurted. "You're ruining other men for me. No mere mortal can measure up to this." I waved my free hand at his chest as he rose and dusted his hands on his jeans.

"Spanish men have been doing that for years. Don't let the French or Italians fool you. They're amateurs."

I laughed. "Thank you. This is lovely."

"You are most welcome, Doña Natividad." He bowed. "Did your friends find evidence of the afterlife?"

"No. One blur and a few bumps they claim are footsteps. I'm not impressed."

"Well I hope that you find this setting more rewarding." Cris gestured to our surroundings. "We have three gardens. A kitchen garden for herbs and vegetables, a rose garden, and a wildflower garden. This is the rose garden, as you may have guessed. It is my favorite place."

"It's beautiful." I'd never seen so many varieties of roses in my life, but my flower education was sorely lacking. I had a black thumb—houseplants wither in terror when I pass by. I walked the twisting stone paths, my skirt flowing around me like a fairy-tale princess. The smell was amazing—damp and earthy from the days of rain, but still the best perfume I'd encountered. No wonder the scent clung to Cris. The petals sparkled in the sunlight thanks to the dew that hugged the blooms. It was a shame that winter was about to ruin their beauty.

"You do all this by yourself?" I asked.

"Yes."

"Just you and Diego?"

He opened and shut his mouth as though about to say something but thinking better of it, and he cleared his throat. "Yes. He supervises. It is too difficult for him to garden now."

I nodded and swallowed the urge to ask what his plans were after the manor was sold. It wasn't my business, and it had to be a tender subject.

I returned to my wandering. I glanced at Cris a few times, hiding my regard beneath my dark lashes. He was intense, his focus homed in on me like a laser as he watched my every move like a hawk. Was he worried that I'd poke the flowers? Or was he really that interested in me? No man had ever watched me with that much interest, not even the ones I'd dated. Then again I'd never really had an intense relationship. Plenty of fun sex, but I'd never had a boyfriend last past the six-month mark.

"Do you like it?" Cris asked.

"It's amazing. I've never seen anything like it."

"You do not have roses in America?" he teased.

"We do. I live in a tiny apartment, smaller than this garden. I don't have any plants."

"You do not like them?" Cris circled closer, like a great cat stalking prey. I really hoped he planned on pouncing on me.

"Plants are fine. I'm not interested in anything I have to take care of, and I'm away for long periods of time."

"You don't believe in putting down roots?"

"My roots are in Chicago. I'm happy visiting them during major holidays." I still considered Chicago home, even though I hadn't lived there since I graduated with my bachelor's degree. My parents' phone number was listed as "home" in my contacts.

"Tell me of your favorite place there." He brushed a lock of hair from my face.

"Millennium Park."

"A garden?" he asked.

"Sort of. My favorite spot in the park is called the Crown Fountain. A Spanish artist designed it, in fact, from Barcelona. It's these two giant pillars that are covered with videos of different faces, and every few minutes the faces spit water onto the kids playing between them. My nieces and nephews *love* it. It's wall-to-wall kids, all playing and splashing together, having a blast. We go every year when I visit for the Fourth of July."

Cris studied me as he wound a lock of my hair around his finger. "You come from a large family?"

"I'm the eldest of seven."

"Why haven't you married? You're beautiful, successful. Intelligent. A man would be blessed to have you as his wife."

I opened my mouth to argue in reflex—not about being marriage material, but because I'd been raised to be a Good Girl, and good girls were modest. Good girls never admitted to being beautiful. But working in television had taught me that you didn't argue with people who complimented you. You smiled and thanked them.

"Thank you, but I enjoy my freedom. I like being able to travel and see the world. Have adventures. Meet dark, handsome strangers." I grinned, and he stroked the curl around his finger. Lust fluttered in my belly like an amorous butterfly.

"You aren't afraid of having your heart broken by one of these handsome strangers?" he asked.

"No. I just use them for sex." I winced—it sounded crass when put that way. Honest, but crass.

"I am happy to volunteer for that," he teased.

I blushed. "Thanks, but I don't want you to think that I feel entitled to you, like you're an amenity that comes with the house. I've had to put up with that myself when I was working as an assistant. There are a lot of jerks who think their assistants should be offering them more than coffee."

He frowned, his brow furrowed. "I'm sorry you were treated in such a way."

"Why aren't you married?" I blurted. "I bet women swoon when you walk by."

Cris grinned, but there was a sadness in the expression. "It has been known to happen, though not often as of late. I envy you your freedom. I am tied to this land." He sighed, but then he took my hand and raised it to his lips, pressing a gentle kiss against my knuckles. "I am flattered that you are concerned for my honor. Enjoying each other's company would be more entertaining, but I agree that it may be best to keep our relationship professional, given the circumstances."

Did I want that? Not even a bit. But despite the thirsty demands of my libido, my brain was still functioning well enough to recognize that I hadn't reached the minimum amount of trust and comfort with this situation to jump him. Not yet at least.

"Thank you." I reluctantly glanced back at the manor. "I should go. I want to get some research in before I have to commune with the spirits again."

"Of course. Happy hunting." He grinned, and I shook my head as I retreated.

I stopped in the kitchen for a quick snack, then took a plate of olives and cheese to the library with me. The library was amazing, a two-story fantasy of leather-bound books and collected curiosities. I inhaled the scent of old books and felt at home. I hoped to find some local history contained in the massive collection, but my plans were almost immediately derailed when I discovered an old leather-bound copy of *Don Quixote*. I spent the remainder of my snack time tilting at windmills instead of researching, and by the time I returned to the kitchen, the sun had already set.

With a full stomach and a skeptical mind I arrived at the command center and called the team. "So what's on the menu for tonight?"

John frowned at me. "Where have you been?"

"You guys are watching my every move on camera. I'm pretty sure you know where I've been," I countered.

"Why haven't you checked in?" he asked.

"I was gardening, then reading. Why, did something happen?"

"We found an additional piece of evidence from last night, and I need you to look into it."

Ugh, not more light anomalies. "Okay. What is it?"

"At the same time we caught one of the sets of footsteps we caught your bedroom door opening and closing."

I frowned. "You're not filming my bedroom."

"No, but we have a camera shooting down that hallway."

"But the door opens inward, and it was pitch black. How could you tell if it opened?"

"Here, I'll show you the footage." John brought up another clip of grainy IR camera footage. This clip was even less convincing than the "shadow man" they claimed to see earlier. All that was visible was a faint movement on the wall across from my room which might have been made by the door opening and closing. Or it could be a simple camera glitch, but was most likely wishful thinking on the team's part.

"I'm still not seeing it," I admitted.

"Do you sleepwalk?" John asked.

"I did when I was little. My mother kept finding me trying to unlock the front door and leave. But considering how loud Connie snored that was probably self-preservation."

The team chuckled. John shushed them. "But you don't do it anymore?"

I shrugged. "No idea. I live by myself, so there's no one to witness if I do."

"I volunteer as tribute," Kenji yelled in the background.

"In your dreams, nerd," I replied. The team emitted a chorus of "Ooh"s and one "Sick burn."

"I want you to take a handcam and film yourself testing the door. See if it opens easily, or sticks. The latch could be broken. Did you lock it last night?"

"No. Should I? It's just me here. Do ghosts pick locks?"

The jury was split on that one. John finally said, "Ghosts can't. Demonic entities can."

"What's with this demonic entity stuff?" I asked. "And shadow people? How is that different from a ghost?"

John frowned, his brow furrowed with concern. "On the show we focus on hauntings by human spirits because the producers like the historical connections. But in our downtime we also investigate demonic activity, which is caused by inhuman spirits. It can be very dangerous."

"Like how dangerous?" I asked.

"People have died. Gone insane. This is bad shit, Nati. I'm not joking here. There's been a big uptick in demonic activity across the country. Europe could be affected too."

I blinked—John never swore. He was the most even-tempered person I knew, and he never got upset. I chewed my bottom lip as I pondered what that meant. I didn't believe in any of this, but John did, and he was seriously worried about me. Maybe it was finally time to tell him that I was an atheist—though they were recording this, and if footage got back to my mother there would be epic hell to pay.

"So by demons you mean real, Old Testament demons. Like cast out of Heaven and all that jazz," I said.

"Yes."

"What should I do?" I asked. "Find a cross? I'm sure there's one around here somewhere."

I frowned, because come to think of it, for a house full of knickknacks it was light on religious imagery, and that struck me as odd. My parents' house had at least one crucifix and Madonna in every room, including the bathrooms. It's really unnerving to have the Blessed Virgin watch you pee.

"Don't provoke anything," John advised. "If you see any weird shadows, tell us immediately. If you have any weird scratches or bruises, tell us that too."

I hid my blush behind a gulp of bottled water. Sure I had scratches and bruises, and I knew exactly how I'd gotten them. "All right. I'll go look at the door now."

# CHAPTER FIVE

I spent a half hour opening, closing, poking and prodding my bedroom door. The verdict was that there was absolutely nothing remarkable about the door. It creaked very faintly but didn't stick, and the lock worked just fine. It didn't swing shut, or open for that matter. I promised the team that I would set up the handcam in the hallway, lock the door and put a chair in front of it before I went to bed, and we proceeded with the night's investigation.

They sent me to the ballroom first, where there were reports of phantom dancers and eerie music. Visions of the Haunted Mansion in Disneyland waltzed through my head as I entered and set gadgets around the room—a geophone to catch the vibration of ghostly dancing feet, the S3, an EMF meter, the thermal camera. So many beeping, blinking things, but all were silent at the moment.

"Dance," Piper ordered.

"I am not dancing on national television."

"You're not on national television, it's just us here."

"It's not national television *yet*," I countered. "You know the show is going to use this in some sort of very special 'punish the nonbeliever' episode. Besides, I am not dancing in front of Kenji."

"Hey!" Poor Kenji, always the butt of the joke. He'd thank me later.

"You're in the ballroom. If you dance you may stir up activity," Piper said.

I put my hands on my hips as I glared at the stationary IR camera. "There's a Dead Can Dance joke in there somewhere, just waiting to happen. Okay. I'm going to turn off the voice recorder, and turn on something to dance to on my tablet."

I had a collection of flamenco music in my playlist—it seemed fitting for a trip to Spain—and I chose one of the tracks. I'd traded my long skirt for a pair of jeans, because I'd learned from watching footage of Piper that the IR lighting wasn't kind to women's clothing. My attempt at dancing would've looked better in the skirt, but it wasn't half bad. I'd taken a few ballroom dancing classes in high school and swing dancing in college. I twirled a few times, and then switched to salsa, because I was in the mood to shake my hips.

The geophone and EMF meter burst into beeping life, and I stopped. The lights flickered for a few moments more and then vanished. I stared at them—tremors, maybe? Vibrations traveling through the wooden floor? Had to be.

"Try dancing again," Piper suggested.

"Do they make you dance on the show?" I asked.

"No, but I bet they will now. Suck it up, buttercup."

"Gee, thanks."

I tried a different tactic. I switched songs on my tablet to the habanera from *Carmen,* flipped my headset's mic out of the way and began singing along. Again, I wasn't bad—years of concert choir at our local church. After the second verse the electronics began to light up like Christmas. Piper murmured "Whoa" in my ear and encouraged me to keep going. So I did. When I reached the end of the aria, Piper directed me to a cold spot that had formed across the room. I pointed the digital thermometer at it and shook my head in disbelief.

"It's twenty degrees colder in this spot." What the actual fuck?

"That's what the thermal says too. The spot formed when you were singing. It's sort of blobby, about four feet high."

*Bullshit.* They had to be messing with me. I stuck my hand out to touch it but felt nothing. I fetched the thermal camera and watched the cold spot move.

"I think...I think it's doing a box step," I said. Great. Day two of paranormal investigating and I'd joined team crazy. There was a weird sort of logic to it; made more sense than a roving air vent in a building that didn't have air vents. I searched the room for logical sources of the cold spot, like cracks in the plaster.

"It's gone," Piper informed me on my second circuit of the room. "Try doing an EVP session."

I traded the thermal camera for the DVR and switched it on. I started with the standard questions, talking to thin air, and the S3 blurted out a word and scared the hell out of me.

"BYE LA," it droned in its creepy computer voice. If it asked if I wanted to play a game of chess I was going to smash it with a hammer.

I squeaked and almost dropped the recorder, making sure to mark with spot with, "Nati freaked out." When my heart stopped trying to pound its way out of my chest I cleared my throat. "*Baila*," I corrected. "It means dance. You guys didn't program this thing for multiple languages?"

"Umm...apparently not," Piper said.

"You're telling me that you all seriously believe that everyone speaks English in the afterlife?" We were having a long talk about white American privilege when I got back.

"CONE ME GO."

"*Conmigo*. With me. Dance with me. Cute." My heart kicked back into overdrive. The team had to be feeding it text through the Wi-Fi. They were just fucking with me. The column of cold air couldn't be a spirit. There was a completely rational explanation for it, and I just hadn't found it yet.

"I don't believe in ghosts," I muttered.

"This is why we use scientific methods and not mediums and

Ouija boards," Piper said matter-of-factly. "No one believed in gravity once, or that the earth was round. Half the Senate still doesn't believe in climate change."

I scowled. "But we stopped believing in the supernatural when we started believing in science. The two don't go together."

"Says who?"

*Reason.* I set my jaw before insulting Piper. She was quirky but not unreasonable. Plenty of people believed in what they couldn't see—like my diehard Catholic mother, who had forced me to participate in the church choir for all those years. She thought prayer solved everything. I'd yet to see prayer do anything but waste a perfectly useful Sunday morning.

It had to be the team. They were feeding words to the gadget to inspire interesting television. Fine. I'd play along. After all, I was getting paid well for this.

"What's next on the itinerary?" I asked, changing the subject.

"We're going to investigate where that shadow figure was seen."

"I thought John said not to poke the shadow figure?"

"We're not poking. We're investigating," Piper said. "Besides, you don't believe in these things, right?"

"Right." I did not believe in ghosts. I believed in promotions, bonuses and PhDs. I closed my eyes for a moment and imagined what colors I'd paint the walls of my future condo.

I soldiered on.

Most of the team's investigations were a few minutes of action that took place over several hours of investigating. It functioned well enough for a TV show—they had an hour time slot, which worked out to about forty-two minutes of show and the rest commercials. Plus there was the intro, the history of the place, the team setup, and then the review and reveal at the end of the show. A few episodes covered two sites when paranormal activity was scarce.

After I left the ballroom I spent two solid hours wandering

around the pitch-black manor with absolutely no responses. Boring as hell, and I stubbed my toe on a vicious end table. Finally convinced that we should move on, the team talked me through setting up new equipment. I lined the hallway outside my bedroom with a series of rem-pods—fat little canisters packed with vibration, electromagnetic field and temperature detectors.

"Now what?"

"We have a list of requests for you to sing next," John said.

"If I sing them, will I be excused from investigating the cellar?" I asked.

"No."

"Then no."

"I have movement on camera three," Kenji said.

My brow furrowed as I tried to remember which one was three and where it was located. Shit. It was right here, at the end of the hallway. The rem-pods triggered one by one in time with the *thump, thump, thump* of approaching boot steps, and my breath caught in my throat.

How was this possible? The gadgets triggering I could explain, because I was one hundred percent sure it was possible for the team to control them remotely to instill a little fear of the paranormal in me. But the heavy footfalls were sharp and clear and I could feel the vibration of each step thrum through the soft rubber soles of my shoes, like the ominous warning of an approaching T. rex. The team couldn't fake that. Not without some sort of machinery that would show up on the thermal, or to the naked eye. My mind scrambled for sane explanations. Plumbing? Hot water pipes?

The footsteps stopped just out of arm's reach. My racing heart leaped into my throat. It stopped—why did it stop? Wouldn't water through the pipes keep going past me, continuing down the line? I waited and counted silently, like a child counting the beats between lightning and thunder to determine the nearness of a storm. *One one thousand, two one thousand...*

When I hit thirty seconds I swallowed hard. "What do I do?" I whispered to Piper.

"Turn on the spirit scanner. It's great at picking up—" she started, but then the S3 in my bag blurted a word. The sound was muffled by the leather, so I pulled it out and read the screen in the faint light from the handcam's display.

"KNOTTY."

"Knotty?" I repeated. Then I swallowed hard. *Nati.* The S3 had just said my name. "Piper! I swear to God if you jerks are texting shit to this thing I will beat the shit out of all of you. Okay, maybe not you, because of the baby," I babbled. "I'll kick Kenji's ass twice."

"Hey!" Kenji protested in the background.

"Nati. Focus," Piper said. "Ask it a question. Who is it? What does it want?"

"I don't want to know."

"Yes you do." Piper's voice was calm and soothing, probably channeling that irritating "motherhood has made me wise" energy that my sisters had all used on me. "You are a researcher. Questions are your life. Ask one."

Right. I breathed a ragged, shuddering breath and struggled for calm. This was silly. Ghosts weren't real. I was letting the team goad me into some sort of psychological episode brought on by the darkness, my isolation and the general forlorn atmosphere of the estate. I was tougher than this.

"Okay. Who are you?" I asked.

I stared at the S3's tiny screen and watched the cursor blink. Nothing. Maybe the team felt guilty for giving me a panic attack.

"What do you want?"

Silence. Good.

I don't know what possessed me to turn at that moment. There must have been some movement in my peripheral vision, something that triggered my instinct to turn and face it. Standing beside me, close enough to touch, was the shadow man. My brain struggled to process it—a human form, taller and broader than me, solid but completely comprised of darkness—but then my thought process blue screened like an ancient computer running Windows 95. I screamed and bolted as fight-or-flight adrenaline surged through my veins. I tore to the end of the dark hallway and slapped the lights on, and there was nothing there.

"Nati?" Piper said.

"What the fuck was that?" I shouted.

"Ow. Calm down," she admonished. "What did you see?"

"The shadow man was right next to me. Right! Next! To me!"

"Turn the lights off and film it!"

"Are you crazy?" I snapped. Was I crazy? Had all of this investigating nonsense gone to my head? My hand trembled over the light switch as I struggled to decide what to do next.

"Nati, our team runs *toward* the activity, not *away* from it."

"And you're never bloody alone in a haunted house, are you? It's you, and a partner investigator, and the camera man and a sound guy—" I babbled. I was about to launch into a reminder of how I was absolutely alone in a foreign country where serial killers and/or human traffickers could be waiting to pounce on me and help would never get here in time. But then the rem-pod nearest where I had seen the shadow man triggered, blinking and beeping in the bright light of the hallway. A second pod alarmed, closer, as though headed in my direction, and I bolted again. I slapped on lights as I went, all the way back to the command center. Then I threw the door open, switched the lights on in there, and locked all the doors. I even hauled dining chairs away from the table to blockade them.

"You're overreacting," Piper said. I ripped the headset off and grabbed a poker from the set next to the fireplace.

"I am not overreacting," I yelled at the empty room. I clutched the poker and strained to hear the sound of approaching footsteps.

I don't know how long I stood there looking like an idiot, but my fingers ached from clutching the poker's iron handle by the time I set it down next to the monitors. I checked each camera for movement, but all was quiet in the house. I started to scroll back the footage of what had happened in the hallway, when suddenly the S3 spoke from where I'd shoved it back in my bag.

I yelped and leaped out of the chair, brandishing my poker again. With my free hand I reached into the bag and read the screen: "KNOTTY. MINE."

Mine? Was the shadow man claiming ownership of me? If it was a demon, did that mean it was after my soul? I'd never longed so much for a set of rosary beads in my life.

"Leave me alone!"

I shut the S3 off before it could continue to further scare me shitless. I pulled up the music app on my tablet—after flipping off the team, who was waving soundlessly at me on the screen, trying to get my attention, and ending the call—and I started my Christmas playlist. It was the closest I was going to get to religious music.

With the speakers blasting Mariah Carey's "Silent Night," I returned to the camera feeds, watching for intruders—normal or paranormal.

## CHAPTER SIX

"Nati?"

My eyes flew open and I squealed and jerked away, tumbling out of the chair and landing on the dining room floor with an awkward thud. Cris stared at me for a wide-eyed moment, then knelt at my side and checked for injuries.

"What happened? Are you hurt?" he asked.

"How did you get in?" My mouth was gritty as though I'd chugged wet sand. I wiped my lips—oh God, had Cris seen me drooling? Was there a puddle on the table next to the keyboard?

"I am the caretaker. I have keys," he reminded as he helped me sit up. "Plus, next time you barricade a door, make sure to check whether the door swings outward or in." He cocked a thumb over his shoulder in the direction of the servants' entrance.

"Oh." My legs were rubbery as I stood, and then I threw my arms around him. "I was so scared." I buried my face in his chest.

"I gathered that." He rubbed my back as I clung to him. "What happened?"

"The demon was right next to me and it said my name!" I winced, sure I sounded like a complete lunatic.

Cris patted my hair comfortingly. "Demon? I thought you were hunting ghosts? I have never heard of a demon at Mendoza Manor."

"The team said that shadow people were demons...I sound insane. I need coffee."

"No, you need rest. Did you sleep here?"

"I tried to stay awake until sunrise. I guess I fell asleep near the end."

He tsked and shook his head. "I will escort you to your room, and you can tell me all about your adventure after you are rested."

I nodded—very reasonable. At least one of us was still sane. Cris offered me his arm like an old-world gentleman, and I smiled as I took it. He walked me to my room and brushed a chaste kiss across my cheek.

"Rest well, Natividad. Know that you are safe here."

I slept like the dead—deep and dreamless. I rolled out of bed around two o'clock, indulged in a hot shower and a large cup of coffee, and then wandered outside to look for Cris. He wasn't in the rose garden, and as I hovered at the garden's edge and debated where to go next, a flash of white caught my eye. It was there for an instant and then gone, like the white tail of a deer disappearing into the woods after dashing away from the highway. What had Cris been wearing when he found me that morning? It might have been a white T-shirt. I liked that explanation better than an apparition wandering the grounds during daylight hours. It could happen—after all, that was why the team had insisted on rolling the cameras nonstop during my stay.

Jesus. Two nights of investigating and I'd joined the dark side. I needed to get my shit together.

I headed in that direction, following instinct more than anything else. After I walked a few feet past the tree line, I found a small but well-worn path that led me to Angela's grave. I picked my way past the overgrown rosebushes and stood at the base of her monument. I touched the angel's bare foot, and the stone was cold beneath my palm. The marble angel still looked as though it was shedding grimy tears, and I brushed leaves away from the base.

"Diego wants me to help you find peace," I said. "I have no idea how to do that. Peace has never really been my thing, you know? Big city, big family..." I trailed off. "But I'm good at research and uncovering the past. If you could slide me a few hints, or clues, I can handle the rest."

"Nati?"

I yelped and whirled to find Cris standing outside the ring of pointy rosebushes. "You scared me."

"My apologies. Are you all right? How do you feel?"

"Better. A little silly. And guilty."

He quirked an eyebrow. "Why guilty?"

"I'm a lapsed Catholic, I'm an expert at guilt." I smiled dryly. "I'm supposed to be a professional, and I freaked out like a Girl Scout beside a campfire listening to a ghost story. It's stupid."

"You were afraid. There is no shame in that."

"I was buying into the story, and because of that my mind played tricks on me. I'm supposed to be smarter than that." I scowled and shook my head. With careful steps I wove my way to his side. "It's one of the first things we learn when studying history—not to fall for local legends and superstitions."

"Oh?"

I nodded. "There's always a deeper truth that inspired the story. It's a historian's job to discover that truth." I turned and peered at the marble angel. "Something happened here. Something traumatic enough to inspire the family to build Angela this shrine. Why is it so close to the house, but still alone? Why aren't there other family members buried here? Why wasn't she buried with her family, in their plot?"

"I'm afraid I cannot say."

I turned back to Cris and smiled. "I don't expect you to have the answers. But there is something you could help me with."

He bowed. "Of course. I am at your service."

My hormones cracked my melancholy mood with suggestions of ways he could service me, and I cleared my throat. "Would you help me clean this spot up? I have no idea how to help a restless spirit, but tending to her memorial might help me. I need an activity that is outdoors and away from the cameras. And..."

"And?" he prompted.

"It bothers me that she was forgotten. Restoring her memorial is sort of like restoring a piece of her history."

He nodded and peered at me, his head tilted as he regarded me silently. I couldn't quite identify the emotion, but his gaze was intense.

"That is very kind of you." His expression softened and he smiled. "Do you have gardening experience?"

"Well...no. My mother says I'm a menace to plantlife."

"Nonsense. Here," he said, offering me his arm. "Walk with me, and we will devise a plan of action."

We made a slow circuit of the area, and under Cris's expert tutelage I learned to recognize several local weeds—the names sounded exotic in Spanish—and the best method for removing them. He listed the tools we would need, and the tasks we should start with. It was a refreshing change from all the paranormal nonsense the team pestered me with.

"What frightened you so badly last night?" he asked.

I sighed. "I thought I saw... It doesn't matter. It wasn't real."

"What wasn't?" he prodded.

"The team's worked up about there being some kind of shadow demon lurking in the halls. It's ridiculous."

"It is only natural to be frightened when you're alone in a strange place."

"Sure, but it's not natural to be afraid of figments of my imagination. Ghosts aren't real. Or demons. I *know* that, but I think I see one shadowy figure and I run away like a kid scared of monsters under the bed." I shook my head in disgust and tore a spindly weed into tiny pieces.

"Did this shadow creature try to harm you?"

"No."

"Did it try to grab you? Growl at you?"

"No."

"Perhaps it was as afraid of you as you were afraid of it."

I laughed. A demon afraid of me? Not likely. "I'm not scary."

"You are a stranger in its home." Cris shrugged. "Think of it like a house cat. The cat is walking around its home, looking for mice, and then boom! It runs into a strange person in the hallway. It might be startled and hiss, it might even swat at you, but it's more likely to run away."

"I hadn't thought of it that way...but that doesn't make me a believer in demons."

"Demons." He snorted and shook his head. "Why would the manor have demons? Ghosts I could understand, for many generations have been born and died there. But demons? Why?"

"I don't know either. I was sure I saw someone standing next to me, but my night vision is pretty bad." I sighed and tossed my shredded weed away into the trees.

"You are right that it was likely your imagination at work, but should it run away with you again I suggest you embrace your inner historian. Think of it as a witness to interview, nothing more."

"That's a good idea." I nodded and studied Angela's marble angel. Had it been carved to look like her? It seemed young, even delicate. "Eighteen years old. That's hardly enough time to live. I try not to think about what eighteen was like."

"It can't be that long ago for you," Cris said.

"You're sweet, but I'm thirty-three."

"Ah. Yes, that is positively ancient," he said gravely. He laughed as I swatted his arm.

"It's not that. I don't have a problem with my age. I have a problem with what I went through at eighteen." I scowled and rubbed my face with my hands as though I could scrub the memories away. "I learned the hard way what happens when people keep secrets. Ignorance is a dangerous thing. But at least I lived through it. Angela wasn't that lucky."

Cris nodded slowly. "There is a melancholy about this place. Tragedy in an innocent life being cut short."

"The team thought they caught the sound of a woman weeping on my first night."

Cris's brow furrowed as he frowned, appearing disquieted by that news. "She would have cause to weep," he murmured. He straightened, dusting his hands on his jeans. "Let us return to the manor. We can begin our work here tomorrow."

"I wish you could stay with me tonight."

"As do I, but that would violate the terms of the agreement."

I nodded. "At least walk me to the firing squad. The team is going to kill me for freaking out and ignoring them last night."

"I am sure that they will understand. They must have been novice investigators once, yes?"

"Yeah. I feel like I let them down."

"You were alone and afraid. They should not fault you for that."

I nodded and followed him. We washed the dirt from our hands in the kitchen and then he led me to the command center. We stopped outside the main entrance to the dining hall, and Cris took my hand and kissed it. The gesture appeared polite, but the heat in his eyes when he gazed at me over my knuckles made my pulse race. I licked my lips and watched him leave.

The Christmas music was still playing when I entered and I winced. Hopefully the team had muted their headphones and didn't listen to it all day. I stopped the player and picked up my headset. John's stoic visage greeted me when I connected the call.

"I apologize for my unprofessional behavior last night," I started. "You are all trained investigators, and I was not prepared for that experience."

"I understand," John said. I blinked in surprise, because I'd been bracing for the worst. "We've asked a lot of you. Are you okay? We were all worried when we couldn't reach you."

"I was shaken, but I feel better now. Did you catch anything on film?"

"Yes...are you sure you want to see it? It might be easier for you to continue if you don't."

I swallowed hard. That didn't sound good. "Yeah. Show me."

"It's damn fast, so we're going to frame by frame it," John explained.

Green and gray footage popped onto my screen. Damn. I really did look awful in the infrared lighting. Everyone did. It was a wide shot from the camera at the end of the hall. One moment I was staring at the rem-pods going off, and then I began to turn. There, for two frames, a figure stood next to me. No distinct features—it didn't have a face or genitalia, no clothing, just darkness that was solid and had form. Then it was gone, and I took off like a frightened rabbit.

I gnawed on my bottom lip until a taste of blood warned me that I'd bitten through skin.

"But it just stood there, right?" I asked. "It didn't make a grab for me. There aren't any unearthly growls or glowing red eyes?"

"No, it was very quiet. The activity seemed benign, no mal intent."

"So it's not dangerous?"

"Well, it's not Casper the Friendly Ghost, but it doesn't appear to be hostile. We're going to proceed with caution. And I want you to carry a flashlight with you. No more running blind through dark hallways. You can break your neck that way."

"Okay. Where do we go from here?"

# CHAPTER SEVEN

We started with Angela. The team had decided that it was safest not to draw the attention of the shadow man and to focus on contacting Angela's spirit. I wasn't sold on the idea that we had actually made contact with Angela. Granted, my paranormal knowledge was spotty, but Piper had explained the difference between residual hauntings—where the activity played over and over, unchanged, like a recording—and intelligent hauntings, where the spirit was capable of answering questions and interacting with the living. The EVP of crying and the activity in the ballroom could be residual. But chasing after Angela meant I didn't have to worry about the shadow man, so I went along with the team's plan.

"Should I try investigating at her grave?" I asked.

"Are there reports of activity there?" John asked.

"Not that I know of, but it is right next to the property. Apparently the cemetery was once part of the Mendoza land and they donated it."

John pondered the idea while sipping from a mug of coffee with the *Spirit Seekers* logo. "Graveyards are iffy for activity. Better stick with the room she was killed in for now."

Better known as my bedroom. Good thing I was anal about

keeping my room clean. My mother had insisted that everyone old enough to walk make their bed in the morning, and I'd learned that any clothing left lying around would be absconded by my little sisters, who seemed to think that my clothes were so much cooler than theirs.

I set up a geophone at the end of the hallway, a rem-pod outside my door and a handcam and the thermal camera on the dressing table. The S3 was banished to the command center, because I didn't want it blurting anything else creepy. The team, however, had something even worse in mind.

"We want you to use the spirit speaker."

I scowled at John's image on my tablet, propped up next to the cameras on my dresser. "I hate that thing. It's so loud. And the noise is like nails on a chalkboard."

"It's just white noise," Piper commented from off screen. The office chairs were aggravating her back, so the boys had brought in a couch for her and she was reclining out of view.

"Irritating white noise." I scowled as I fished the gadget in question out of my bag. It looked innocent enough—a rectangular black box about the size of an old flip cell phone, attached to a round portable speaker that had been meant for use with an iPod.

"Explain to me why this speaker needs to be turned to eleven?" I glowered at it.

"Because it helps to hear the voices in real time. They're faint, and that's why the human ear can't catch them but sensitive electronic equipment can, hence the term Electronic Voice Phenomenon. If you don't turn the speaker up, you'll miss it in the noise while the device is scanning other frequencies."

They had an explanation for everything. "Okay. How does it work?"

"Cover the speaker while you ask your question, like hold it against your leg to muffle the sound, and then uncover it when you're ready for an answer."

Pretty sure I was never going to be ready for an answer from the other side. I wasn't even sure there was an other side. I'd always thought it was wishful thinking—that some eternal reward awaited us after we'd sucked it up through all the blood, sweat and tears we toiled through during life. Made more sense to me to gather your rosebuds while you could while time was still a-flying...

Rosebuds. My thoughts strayed to delicious fantasies about Cris, and I cleared my throat. I turned off the lights and fired up the spirit speaker. It erupted into the hissing, chugging noise that the team called "sweeps." Flinching, I winced and jammed the speaker against my thigh and muffled it with my jeans.

"I'm going to start in Spanish. If the speaker spits out anything in Spanish in reply I'll translate," I said.

"Go ahead," John said over the headset.

Once again I politely introduced myself to Angela and explained that I was descended from her brother, and how I would greatly appreciate it if she would please communicate with me because I wanted to help her. Then I started with a few, simple control questions, like "Can you tell us your name?" and "Where are we right now?"

Nothing. Fifteen minutes of nothing, and then I turned it off to give my ringing ears some peace.

"I'm starting to miss the creepy Speak n' Say," I joked.

"We could try it next," John suggested.

"Not unless you've figured out how to upload a Spanish dictionary to it."

"Point...you know we could really use an investigator fluent in a second language while Piper's on maternity leave," John said.

"Pretty sure I'll be happy to never do this again when my two weeks are up."

"Aww, come on, Nati," Piper spoke up. "It's awesome being a D-list reality TV celebrity. I even had the producers of *Dancing with the Stars* ask after me before I got pregnant."

"Really?" Kenji said. "They didn't talk to me."

"Because they know you have two left feet," John said. We all chuckled, and I smiled. This was why I loved the team, even though they were wacky ghost hunters. They were good people, their own odd family. They looked after each other. It made them fun to watch. When other reality shows were screaming and throwing drinks at each other, the *Spirit Seekers* team was joking around and having a good time.

"I'm not celebrity material, of any grade."

"You don't want fame and fortune?" Piper asked.

"Do you?" I asked.

It was silent, and then Kenji popped into view on the tablet's screen. "She's doing that creepy belly-rubbing thing while grinning like a maniac."

I laughed. "It's not creepy. It's a nesting thing. My little sisters both went through it. They'd stare into space like they were communing with the mother ship."

"See? Creepy," Kenji said. "Wait, your little sisters have kids and you don't?"

"Yeah. I'm too busy babysitting you guys to have my own."

Kenji lost the battle to contain a goofy grin. "Well, if you need help with that I'd be happy to volunteer."

"In your dreams, dork," I replied.

A chorus of "Ooh"s and a "Do you need to apply cold water to that burn?" sounded through the headset.

Kenji simply shrugged. "Just thought I'd ask."

"Okay, break time's over, kids," John said. "Let's get back to the Q&A."

I turned on the noisy box and started the questions again, but this time I was distracted. I was the oldest in my family, and the rest of my siblings were married, with children. The holidays were loud, raucous insanity. Fine in small doses, but I liked the freedom of being single and childless.

Didn't I? I had no intention of budging on the kids issue, but would it be so terrible to have someone to see the world with? Or come home to? Someone to make me Spanish omelets every morning?

"*Novia*," the speaker spit out. It was a woman's voice, weak as though whispering from across the room.

I almost missed it, and John prompted me. "What did it say?"

"*Novia*," I repeated. "Means girlfriend, or bride. Were you killed on your wedding day?"

"*Sí*."

Holy shit. This was happening. Really, actually happening. I swallowed hard, dizzy and lightheaded. This was a turning point, the moment before the fall. I could either keep fighting or dive in.

What the hell? If you can't beat 'em...

"Who killed you?" I asked.

A long pause, then, "*Sombra*."

"Shadow," I translated. A chill shivered down my spine. I covered the speaker. "Do you think she means the shadow man? Can they really kill people?"

"It's possible."

"What did the shadow do?" I uncovered the speaker and held my breath.

"Sangre."

Blood. My heart raced as a cool breeze brushed over my forearm, like the light caress of a concerned friend. This time I didn't jump or scream—okay, I may have yelped a bit. Then I shut the spirit speaker off and grabbed the thermal camera.

"Nati—" John began.

"Yeah, I see it too." A wispy, purple-blue blob floated in the middle of the screen. It was slow and ponderous, as if every ghostly step took a great effort. Maybe it did. "Are you guys getting anything on the IR cameras?" I whispered, as if afraid that speaking too loudly would scare the spirit away.

"No, just the thermal."

"I have the thermometer in my bag, but I'm afraid I'll drop the camera if I go for it."

"Don't," John said. "That camera costs a fortune. We're good for now."

"Tía Angela. I want to help you," I said. "What can I do?"

I heard soft weeping in reply, and the hair on the back of my neck rose as a chill shivered down to my toes. I froze—the sound hadn't emanated from any of the team's gadgets. I heard it with my own ears, and sadness settled over me like a thick blanket. I blinked as tears stung my eyes.

What the actual fuck?

*Breathe. Slow and easy.* There was no point in freaking out again.

"Did you guys hear that?" I whispered.

"Hear what?" John asked.

"Crying. Check your audio."

I watched the cold blob move back and forth. My mind's eye pictured a young woman wringing her hands as she paced. Murdered on her wedding night. Had she died a virgin? Maybe she'd been frightened of her new husband, who I knew nothing about. Was he older? Had he had other wives? Did he love her? Probably not if he killed her, but why marry her and then kill her in the same day? The guy had to be a real psychopath.

"We didn't catch anything," John said. "That's not uncommon, though. Half of the things we see or hear aren't caught on camera."

I'd always thought that was suspiciously convenient. It seemed like the team was forever spotting apparitions just off-screen.

"There might be something on your audio recorder," Piper said. "We'll check it during our review."

"Right. Now what?" I asked.

"We have movement on the first-floor cameras," John said.

"Which ones?" I glanced at my tablet's screen and did not like John's expression as he stared at his monitor.

"All of them. Shit."

I tensed, unsure of what to do, and suddenly the cold spot zipped out of the camera's view. I fumbled with it as I turned, trying to find where it went, and suddenly the door slammed shut. My jaw dropped as I heard the lock click. With shaking hands I set the thermal camera down on the bed before I dropped the thing, and then I crossed to the switch and slapped on the lights. My eyes stung in the bright light as they struggled to adjust. I reached for the doorknob and it refused to turn, and then I discovered the key was missing.

"Umm, guys?"

They were all talking at once. I retrieved my tablet and frowned at the sight of the team all frantically working at their computers. That couldn't be good.

"Guys?" I said again. "Hello? Little help here."

"Sorry, Nati," John said. "Things just got crazy."

"Define *crazy*." I was very impressed with how calm my voice sounded in comparison to my frantic heartbeat. My hands shook, and I balled them into fists to fight it. Despite the adrenaline fueling my shakes, I felt better with the lights on. I turned the bedside lamps on, too. Just in case.

"There was a ton of movement," Kenji said. "And then the cameras shut off. You have to get down there."

"There's a small problem with that plan." I swapped the camera so it faced out and pointed it at the door. "The door is locked and the key is gone."

"Gone?" John asked. "Did it fall out when the door shut?"

"No, I would've heard it hit the hardwood floor. I heard it lock after it shut." I shifted my grip on the tablet and tried the doorknob again. Nothing.

"Can you pick the lock?" Kenji asked.

"No, I can't pick the lock. Are you serious right now? What kind of question is that?"

"Well, your dad's a cop," he replied.

"Right, and he's not a locksmith." I sighed. "Cris has keys. He can let me out in the morning. What's going on downstairs?"

"No idea," John said. "Everything's off on the whole floor. No audio, no visual, nothing."

"Anything upstairs?"

"Second-floor cameras are all up and running. We're monitoring them now to see if we can hear anything. Do you hear anything?"

"Hang on." I removed my headset and strained to listen. Nothing. "Nada."

"Use the spirit box," John said.

"No. I'm going to take this as a hint and call it a night."

"Aww, come on," Kenji said. "Things just got interesting."

I frowned. "Not really seeing how being locked into my room is interesting. Maybe she was pissed because I'm up past my bedtime."

"Nati," John began, but I cut him off.

"I'm going to keep my phone and my tablet on my nightstand. If anything happens you can call me. Okay?"

He sighed. "Fine."

I ended the call and stared at the screen. Would it contaminate their audio evidence if I played my Christmas music? I decided that I didn't care, and the sounds of Bing Crosby crooning about dreaming of a white Christmas filled the room. I lay down on the bed—fully clothed, all the lights on—and closed my eyes.

Eventually I began to drift off, and as I did I thought I heard a woman softly humming and caught the scent of faded floral perfume.

## CHAPTER EIGHT

I woke to someone knocking on my door.

"Nati?" Cris asked. "Are you all right?"

"Fine." More or less. I winced as I rolled off the bed—my eyes were gummy and my neck was stiff, and I was afraid to glance in the dressing mirror and see what state my hair was in.

"Your team called. They said you are locked in. If I may?"

"Please do."

My heart lifted at the sound of jangling keys and the tumblers turning in the lock. The door opened and I hugged him. "My hero," I mumbled against his chest. "Thank you."

Cris chuckled. "You are welcome. How did you lock yourself in?"

I stepped back and sighed. "I didn't. Tía Angela did, right before all the cameras went down on the first floor. Is everything okay there?"

"To my knowledge, yes, but I did not inspect the equipment." He shrugged. "Everything appears as it did yesterday."

"Huh. Maybe the team caught something."

Cris peered past me and frowned. "Isn't that your room key?"

"Where?" I turned, expecting to see it on the floor in a spot that had been revealed by the morning sun streaming through the windows, but I didn't see it.

"There, on your night table."

My jaw dropped—there, neatly placed beside my phone and the handcam, was my missing room key. Dumbfounded, I crossed to the table and picked it up, and the metal was cool against my skin.

"I should've kept the camera on." I winced and set the key down. "Oh no. I really am becoming one of them. Next I'll be carrying around an EMF detector with me at all times in my purse."

Cris chuckled. "Perhaps you will regain your senses after breakfast, no?"

"Good plan, but I need to shower first." I bit my tongue to stop from inviting him to join me. Professional relationship. Right. I cleared my throat. "I'll see you downstairs. Thanks again."

Cris bowed and grinned. "I am privileged to be your savior."

I laughed and enjoyed the view as he walked away. My savior had a damn fine ass. I felt blessed.

After a hot shower and a change of clothes, I discovered breakfast waiting in the kitchen under a warming plate, complete with a single red rose and a note promising to begin our gardening plan of attack when I was ready. I inhaled the rose's scent with a goofy grin before pouncing on the food.

Refreshed, I entered the command center and called the team. John's image popped into view, and I frowned.

"Did you even sleep?" I asked.

"Not yet." John rubbed his eyes. "We're still doing evidence review."

"Oh! The key," I said. "I found the bedroom key on my nightstand this morning."

I winced as a chorus of "Did you film it?" blasted through the speakers.

"I am not filming my bedroom while I sleep. Period. Hard limit."

John sighed. "Fine. Kenji wants to talk you through inspecting the cameras."

"Sure. Did you find anything before they went down?"

He grimaced, and my stomach dropped because that was not a good sign. "We're still reviewing it. We'll know more after you have a look around."

I synched my headset to my phone and called Kenji for paranormal tech support. There really didn't appear to be anything wrong with the cameras, but they had each been unplugged and their backup batteries completely drained. I reconnected each one and replaced the battery packs. The team cut me loose after that, and Cris and I started our extreme memorial makeover.

The work was dirty, sweaty and bloody—the rosebushes must have been some sort of vampire hybrid, because the thorns clearly had it out for me. But aside from all that, I was glad to have something sane to do. Gardening was one hundred percent spirit free, and I desperately needed that.

A muscle pinched between my shoulder blades and I stopped to stretch it. The weeping angel watched me with her mournful expression, and I scowled. She wasn't the first religious figure to disapprove of me, and I doubted she'd be the last. My throat tightened as a surge of old memories assaulted me.

"Nati? What's wrong?" Cris asked.

I swallowed hard before breathing a shaky breath. "I don't want it to be real."

"How so?" Brow furrowed, he leaned the handle of his rake against a tree trunk.

"If all this supernatural shit is real, and the church is right about everything, then I'm in big trouble. Definitely going to hell. I'm not okay with that."

"Nonsense," Cris scoffed. "You are a good person. You couldn't possibly have done something to deserve such a punishment."

"Agreed, but..." The lump in my throat swelled and threatened to choke me as I struggled for a watery breath. "I had an abortion. The church is pretty clear about their views on it. It's why I left the church and never looked back. Because fuck them." I spat the curse and leaped to my feet, hands balled into fists. "If those assholes had bothered to teach us the basics of contraceptives instead of their abstinence-only bullshit, then Brian would've known the right way to put on a damn condom and it wouldn't have broken. Or I could've had access to the pill without getting my mother's permission, which she never would've granted and would've freaked out because I was sexually active like some sinful Jezebel." I hissed my frustration, grabbed a clump of weeds and hurled it into the trees, where it exploded against a tree trunk in a shower of dirt. "And now she wants me to reconnect with Brian. Fuck."

Cris held his hands up in surrender as he eased closer. "This is why you do not want children?"

"I never wanted children. Helping raise my brothers and sisters was enough for me. I had everything planned out just the way I wanted it, and suddenly I was the screwup who got pregnant her senior year." I pointed a warning finger at him in warning before he got any closer. "Ignorance did this. If I'd been properly educated I wouldn't have had to go through any of that. Everyone deserves to know the truth, but instead of letting me decide what was best for me, I had to deal with everyone else choosing what they thought I needed to know. Keeping secrets ruins lives."

He paused as though considering his next words very carefully, which was a wise move. "I understand. But your life was not ruined. You travel the world and visit interesting places."

"Because I stood my ground." I folded my arms and hugged my chest as though I could squeeze the ache out of it. "She wanted me to have the baby. She wanted me to *keep* the baby. To forget about my college plans and be a wife and mother, like her. I never wanted that life. That was her dream, not mine."

"I see. So you had the procedure."

I nodded. "Because I turned eighteen, and I spent most of my college savings on it. I had to do two years of community college instead of the whole four years at the university, but I managed it.

Mama never really forgave me, but at least she didn't throw me out of the house."

Cris nodded. "May I?" He held his arms out to embrace me, and I nodded my assent. He wrapped his arms around me, and I shook with unshed tears as I leaned into his embrace. He was warm and solid, and he stroked my hair and whispered soothing words.

"I don't want to be punished forever for one mistake," I murmured.

"I understand. More than you know." Cris brushed a kiss against my hair.

"Don't tell me you got a girl pregnant."

"No. I did allow my manhood to lead me, and it turned out to be a poor decision maker."

I smiled, and it eased the pressure squeezing my chest. "That's why it's important to think with your big head and not your small one."

"Small?" Cris sounded greatly offended, and I giggled.

"Sorry. I'm sure it's splendid," I said gravely, and he chuckled.

"Indeed. Songs have been sung of it." He grinned as he released me. "Here, I think we have made enough gardening progress for one day. Let's clean up, and we can continue tomorrow. Weather permitting."

"Right." Today was bright and sunny, but the forecast promised that the rain would return within the next few days.

Cris hauled away debris in a wheelbarrow, bound for the manor's compost heap, and I returned the tools to their proper places in the toolshed. Instead of returning to the house I walked a few laps in the rose garden to clear my head. I tried not to think about the abortion and all the drama associated with it, but it was completely intertwined with my absence of faith. I didn't want to believe in ghosts, because that implied that there was an afterlife. And if there was an afterlife, that opened the door to all of sorts of things I'd rather not think about.

Well, if I was going to hell, I might as well go for the good seats.

I turned and saw Cris regarding me silently. I crossed to him and placed my hands on his shoulders. I studied his expression, searching for disapproval. Judgement. Instead, Cris framed my face with his hands and kissed me until I was weak in the knees.

"Doña Natividad, you are brave, beautiful and clever. You have a good heart. I see nothing in you worth damnation."

"Thank you."

"What do you want?" he asked.

"You," I said without hesitation. "Here. Now. No regrets, no expectations."

"Done." Cris swept me off my feet and carried me away like Rhett and Scarlet O'Hara. I squeaked in surprise and threw my arms around his neck. He carried me to a nearby gazebo—what was the Spanish term for gazebo? The word didn't seem adequate to describe the fantasy of climbing roses, spiraling wrought iron details and hardwood furniture. Damn. Their outdoor furniture was nicer than the stuff in my apartment.

Cris set me on a couch and I set my messenger bag on the floor at my feet. He sat beside me, pulled me atop his lap and deftly unbuttoned my blouse. He tossed the garment atop the coffee table—tea table?—and then quickly unhooked my lacy bra and added it to the pile. Cris murmured his approval as he cupped my breasts, what little breast I had. The first time I'd ever been topless with a boy he'd complained that my girls were too small and that my nipples looked like raisins, instead of the plump pink-topped *Playboy* fantasy he'd expected.

"Perfection," Cris murmured.

"You're sweet, but I'm almost flat as a board."

"Nonsense." Cris suckled one peak for emphasis, and I sighed my approval. "You are a perfect fit for my hands." He nibbled at the taut bud, and then trailed a finger over the curve of my breast. "You have bruises here. Did you fall?"

"No, I..." Blushing, I cleared my throat. "I was overzealous in pleasuring myself."

"Really?" His black eyes smoldered with interest as he studied me. "Are you always overzealous?"

"More so when I'm at home and I have my toys to play with," I admitted.

"What sort of toys?"

I grinned. "I'm not telling." I ground my hips against him, and he moaned as he shifted beneath me. Those jeans had to be killing him right now. Luckily I knew a cure for that. I slid to the floor between his knees and reached for his fly.

"Pity. I am most curious, but a lady needs her mystery." His breath caught as I freed his cock, and I practically purred at my prize. Length and girth—he really was a Spanish god. I stroked his shaft and his head lolled back.

"Looking for insight into how to please me?" I teased.

"I like to make informed decisions. Do you prefer your lovers to leave bruises?"

"It's not the bruises. It's the enthusiasm that leaves them that I enjoy."

I licked the underside of his cock from the dark curls around its base up to the head, then circled my tongue around its tip. He tasted of sweat and arousal, and I inhaled his masculine scent. I ordered him to lift his hips, and I tugged the jeans and his boxer briefs down to his ankles, giving me full access to his sex. I cupped his balls in my left hand and massaged them gently, while with my right hand I stroked his shaft. I took the tip of his cock into my mouth and licked, sucked and teased it. His hips bucked as he touched my hair. Gentle at first, as though afraid his touch would discourage me. I glanced up his body and met his gaze, and my hungry expression spurred him into action. Cris grabbed my hair, all gentle pretenses gone, and he fucked my mouth.

I moaned in approval, the sound muffled by his thrusts. Cris growled my name, the sound somewhere between a prayer and a curse. He pushed me back and lurched to his feet, then gripped my hair again and thrust into my mouth. Deep-throating was one of my talents, so I grasped his hips and held on for the ride. My lace panties soaked through with anticipation as I stared up at him. He was wild with need, consumed with pleasure.

I saw the change come over him, the sharp intake of breath as he teetered on the edge of orgasm. Cris flinched, his entire body tense with the need for release.

"Please," he begged. "Dear God. Nati, please. I can't..."

With a wicked smile I deep-throated him, and he came with a shout. I swallowed him down until he collapsed onto the couch, and I sat back on my heels and grinned as he struggled to catch his breath.

"That was..." he began. I rose and slipped off my jeans and panties, adding them to my pile of discarded clothing. A deliciously naughty thrill shivered through me—I was naked and outdoors. Not that anyone was likely to wander by and see us, considering the secluded location, but it was still shocking to my inner good girl. She wanted to have sex in the dark under a pile of blankets, and here I was in the afternoon sunlight, naked as the day I was born.

"A good start, no?" I set one foot on the couch beside him, giving him a good view of my dripping pussy. Thank God I'd kept up on shaving my legs and trimming my lady bits.

Cris licked his lips. "Yes. Lie back on the chaise, and keep your hands above your head." I stretched out as ordered, and he stood at the foot of the chaise and surveyed my body. "It appears that you were quite enthusiastic. What were you thinking of while you pleasured yourself?"

"You."

"Oh?" He knelt beside the chair and started at my ankle, drawing it up to his mouth and suckling the skin. Ankles and the backs of one's knees were often overlooked erogenous zones, but Cris seemed an expert on the subject.

"Yes." Heat pooled at my core, and my hips bucked in anticipation.

"Will you dream of me again tonight?"

"Definitely."

"Good. Then I hope to give you inspiration for more pleasant dreams."

Cris kissed and licked a sensual path up my leg, then draped it over his shoulder as he buried his face in my sex. I bit my lip to stifle my enthusiasm, wondering how far my voice would travel and if the cameras in the house would pick up the sound. He slid two fingers inside me and I decided I didn't care, and loudly moaned my approval.

His moustache brushed against my swollen labia as he licked and suckled my clit, and I writhed beneath him. He slipped a third finger inside me, further stretching my sex.

"Yes, please," I begged. Consumed by need, I wanted all of him. I cried out as I climaxed. Cris continued, fingers pumping fast and hard, working me to a second, a third, and a shattering fourth orgasm that left my skin flushed and covered in a light sheen of sweat.

Cris drew away, and I was pleasantly surprised to see that he was hard again.

"Hold that thought." I paused to liberate a condom from my bag—condoms might have betrayed me in the past, but I don't leave home without them. I just added an IUD to my contraceptive arsenal as backup in case they broke.

I handed Cris the foil packet and he sheathed himself with the condom, then he gripped the undersides of my knees, pulled my legs wide and thrust his cock inside me. I drank in the sight of the lean line of his body and the play of his muscles as he pounded me hard and fast, and his gaze burned as he watched the bounce of my breasts. My throat was ragged from moaning, but he showed no signs of stopping.

"So beautiful, Natividad," he groaned. "You will dream of this tonight. Of me inside you."

"Yes," I gasped in agreement. Damn, I'd dream of this for

years. Kinky exhibitionist sex with a bronzed Spanish god? Hell yeah. "Come for me, please. I need you."

"Not yet." Cris stretched over me and kissed me. He claimed my mouth with a deep kiss, and I tasted my sex on his tongue. He thrust, and I wrapped my legs around him and tilted my hips to meet him. "Not yet."

I exhaled a shaky breath as he gazed into my eyes. "Why?" I asked. "What do you need?"

"Only you."

I embraced him, holding him tight as he whispered endearments, rather like he had in my dream. These words were sweeter, softer. Cris thrust slowly as though savoring every inch, and I ran my hands up and down his back in a hungry caress.

*Why me?* I swallowed the words before I voiced them, afraid of the answers I might receive in reply. I was pretty. I was convenient and easy. It wasn't fair to expect anything more from him when I didn't have any romantic motivation myself. I didn't have time for romance, especially not with a man in a foreign country that I'd be leaving in two weeks.

I cupped Cris's jaw and turned his face to mine. I kissed him, slow and passionate, matching the simmering heat of the thrust of his cock with the strokes of my tongue. Our gazes locked and the moment sizzled, and then he tensed and moaned against my lips as he came. I shivered and cried out as the pulse of his cock pushed me over the edge into a final climax.

Cris dusted my face with soft, light kisses. I was content to enjoy his attention, mesmerized by the feel of his hair as I ran my fingers through it. His hair was a lighter shade of brown than mine was—sun-kissed with blond highlights where my hair smoldered with red lowlights—and just long enough to give him a sexy, tousled look. I traced the thin beard lining his jaw. He had a sort of stylish goatee that gave him a roguish yet well-groomed look, like a gentleman pirate.

"I should get back to the house," I said.

"You should, yes. Just not yet."

~

Before we parted Cris stepped close and kissed my cheek, then whispered in my ear. "You can dream of me. I will be dreaming of you."

"I will."

I could hardly walk straight by the time I returned to the manor, and it was well worth it. I'd never felt so sexually sated in my life. Whatever they fed the men around here must give them amazing stamina.

I threw together a plate of munchies and headed for the library, determined to finally start researching. I did my best to focus as I scanned the titles that crammed the shelves—I should spend weeks in this library and never get bored, months even. Years...my imagination indulged in the thought of spending every day with Cris. I refused to settle down, but it was nice to daydream about on occasion.

A thump caught my attention, and I turned to see a rolling ladder slide along its track past several bookcases until stopping in front of one I hadn't searched yet. I blinked, afraid to move.

"Tía Angela?" I guessed. No response. I called out to the team. "Guys, I really hope you got that." It might've been within range of the camera that was filming the room, though considering their supernatural batting average it had probably happened just off-screen.

I crossed to the ladder and locked it into place before ascending the stairs. When I reached the top I spied a row of plain leather-bound books with heavily cracked spines, and I squeaked with joy.

"I found ledgers!" I announced. Household ledgers were treasure troves of information. I pulled one to check the dates inside, and then used it as a point of reference to determine which volume was the one I needed. I grabbed it and brought it to the desk.

My phone started vibrating, and I answered it and put it on speaker.

"What is it?" Piper asked.

"Our jackpot." I flipped the cover open and traced my fingers down the page. "It's a record kept by the house steward during the last days of Don Cristóbal Mendoza Ríos, the man who married Angela."

"And killed her," Piper said grimly.

"Hey," Kenji interrupted. "You don't know that. So far all we know is that he disappeared the day she died."

I snorted. "Which means he could've been living on a beach in the New World, drinking rum."

"Or he was killed, too, and they never found his body," Kenji said. Ever the optimist—I'm a pessimist in addition to being a skeptic. Or at least I was before this adventure. The team was rubbing off on me.

I scanned the first few pages and whistled low. "Okay, this is going to take time to translate. The Spanish is...dense. Like Middle English dense."

Piper cursed, and I nodded in agreement.

John spoke up. "We can work on that tomorrow. Right now we need you to head back to the command center so we can show you what we found."

"That good, huh?"

"Let me put it this way," Piper said. "You want to find a cross."

I closed the book and sighed. "Joy. Got it."

"I'm not seeing any of this," I said. The team had concocted an elaborate narrative based on a few seconds of shadowy blurs. According to them, some sort of paranormal throwdown had happened after I was locked in my room, where the shadow man faced off against several other shadow people, *West Side Story*-style. I was moments away from downloading the soundtrack and tormenting them with it.

"Here." Kenji swapped the view on my screen with an image of his monitor. “This is our guy.” He circled the figure like a color commentator about to explain step-by-step how the team scored the winning touchdown. “And these are the intruders.” He circled three squat figures surrounding “our” shadow man.

“Why are they short?” I asked.

“They’re a different type of shadow person,” Kenji said. “They like to masquerade as children.”

Great. Demon children. This just kept getting better. “How do you know they’re intruders? Couldn’t they have been here the whole time?”

“We caught them entering from outside,” John said. Additional video clips replaced Kenji’s play-by-play. Everything still looked like blurs to me.

“And you know this was a fight because...?” I asked.

“Of the audio,” John said.

“Well then you buried the lede,” I scolded. “Play that.”

Silence.

I checked to see if they’d been disconnected, but the call was still live. “Guys?”

“It’s bad, Nati,” Piper said. “This is scary shit.”

Goose bumps shivered down my arms and legs. How bad did it have to be to scare professional paranormal investigators? I rubbed my hands over my arms for warmth and cleared my throat. “It’s okay. Go ahead.”

Unearthly howls, growls and snarls emanated from the speakers, and I’ll admit, I peed a little.

My jaw dropped. “What the actual fuck was that?”

“We’re not sure,” Piper said. “There aren’t any words. It sounds to us like an animal fight.”

“Only if they’re hell hounds,” Kenji said. I heard a thwhap that sounded like Piper had smacked him hard.

Shadow people, demon children and now hell hounds. My stomach twisted into knots and the fruit and cheese I’d snacked on threatened to make a return visit.

"Am I safe here?" I wiped sweaty palms against the thighs of my jeans. More silence. "Hello?"

"We're not sure," John admitted. At least he was honest. "We're getting reports from all over about demon attacks, but so far it's mostly bites and scratches. One broken leg, but he fell down a flight of stairs, so avoid the staircases."

"That's your advice? Stay away from the stairs?" I asked. "That's not comforting."

"We're here with you," John said. "We'll help you deal with whatever happens."

My lips pressed into an unhappy line—they weren't here with me, they were on the other side of the Atlantic Ocean. Once Cris left I'd be completely alone with the things that went bump in the night.

"Well if I'm going to battle the forces of evil, I'm going to need some coffee first. I'll call back in a bit." I ended the call and retreated to the kitchen.

My dark mood lifted at the sight of an enormous bouquet of roses atop the kitchen island. I smiled as I picked up the note left with them—*Dream of me*. Damn right I would. Every step I took stirred a pleasant ache that reminded me of our lovemaking.

*Lovemaking*. Ugh. I couldn't afford to go starry-eyed over Cris. I squared my shoulders and focused on brewing coffee strong enough to slay demons.

We started with Angela again, and apparently she had been waiting for me. The cold spot formed quickly, and then it led me out of the bedroom. It took me to the library and then dissipated as quickly as it had formed. Huh. I scanned the room with the thermal camera, but everything matched room temperature.

"Right...now what?" I asked.

"It must have led you there for a reason," John said. "Are there any paintings from the time period? Portraits of the family, or journals?"

"That ledger is here."

"Try reading aloud from it," John suggested.

I turned and shot a dry look at the IR camera in the library. "You want me to read in the dark? I can't even see my hand in front of my face." I waved my hand for emphasis, and a sigh whispered over the headset.

"Use your flashlight."

I rolled my eyes. "What is this, Girl Scout camp? Will I be making s'mores next?"

"Nati—"

"Fine. Reading by flashlight."

I sat at the desk and propped the thermal camera up so it was aimed at the doorway. I withdrew my flashlight from my bag and opened the ledger.

"I know you all seem to think that Spanish is all the same, but I wasn't kidding when I said this stuff is dense," I warned. "Spain has a whole verb tense that Latin American Spanish doesn't use. And this is a completely different dialect from what I'm used to, and it's handwritten."

"We have faith in your awesome," Kenji said.

I snorted and shook my head. "I should get a raise for this."

Much of it was an account of the needs of the house—servants' wages, food costs, upkeep details—but there were personal notes as well. I skipped to the month before Angela's death and skimmed for details. There were bland notes on wedding preparation details, until the entry dated the day after the wedding.

"Whoa."

"Out loud," Piper shouted.

"I had to find something interesting first, otherwise you'd be listening to commentary on how the local tin peddler is a swindling bastard. And you want the translation, I assume. Unless you understand eighteenth-century Spanish?"

"We love you, Nati," Piper said. "Now read."

"Here goes: Tragedy has struck the household. Yesterday, only hours after the wedding, Doña Angela was discovered murdered. She had been stabbed several times with a knife stolen from the kitchen, suggesting that a servant had committed this foul deed, yet each person was accounted for. Don Cristóbal is missing, and the authorities believe that he killed his bride and fled."

"Nati," John said.

"What?"

"The thermal."

I'd forgotten about the thermal camera. Sick dread settled in my stomach as I looked at the screen, and there in the doorway was a human shape—a large human shape, broad and tall. Fear iced my veins as I froze in terror, but then I remembered Cris's advice to ask it what it wanted.

Right. It's just a big shadowy housecat. It's just as scared of me as I am of it.

Slowly I reached into the bag and withdrew the spirit speaker.

"Don't engage it," John warned.

"I just want to ask it a question," I whispered. I prepared to switch the speaker on. "What do you want?" I asked the shadow.

I switched the gizmo on and held my breath. The horrid hissing static seemed to amplify my anxiety. The voice that emanated from the speaker raised every hair on my body—it was rough and gravelly, the deep bass that one would expect from a demon—but it had a simple message.

"*Ayúdame*." Help me. "*Por favor*." Please.

I blinked, and the shadow vanished, leaving me alone with the noisy sweeps.

"Well," I said as I turned the speaker off. "That was unexpected."

# CHAPTER NINE

The activity vanished after that, and I wandered the house for hours searching in vain. Thankfully the lack of activity meant I could go to sleep at a relatively decent hour. I locked my bedroom door and stowed the key in a drawer in the dressing table, and I moved a chair in front of the door. I doubted that it would keep invading shadow people out, but it was worth a shot.

I stripped naked, crawled into bed and dragged a pillow over my head. Was it silly that I was eager to fall asleep? I felt a bit like a kid at Christmas, but I'd be unwrapping Cris in a sex fantasy as my present and that would definitely put me on the Naughty List. I sighed against the pillow, my skin heating at the memory of our time at the gazebo. Dear God, I'd never had sex that good before, where every inch of me glowed with carnal satisfaction. I had every intention of repeating that performance tomorrow. And the day after that, and the one after that...

I slid my hand between my thighs and stroked my clitoris. A battery-operated toy would've brought a quicker, more reliable result, but the thought of Cris's wicked tongue worshipping my sex brought me to a quick, shuddering climax. I gasped as the orgasm broke over me, and then I curled up on my side and drifted into contented sleep.

"My darling." Cris purred the words as he spooned me, the vibration warm against the sensitive skin just beneath my ear.

Smiling, I wiggled my hips against him, his cock hard against the seam of my ass. His strong arms wrapped around me and my skin practically sizzled at the contact where his body met mine, the steamy flash of heat like stepping into a scalding hot shower.

"I missed you," Cris murmured.

"I see that." I wiggled my hips suggestively and he drew my thighs apart, hooking one leg back over his and spreading me wide. He sheathed himself in my sex in one hard stroke. My back arched as I cried out at the rush of ecstasy.

I pistoned my hips to meet him move for move, pleasure for pleasure. On my side like this I had little access to him, but Cris had full access to me. His hand roamed my body—teasing my nipples, cupping my breasts, then dipping low to massage my clit. He stroked my throat, the span of his hand a light collar pressing against my skin. The gesture was pure dominance—I belonged to him. I shuddered and cried out as ecstasy erupted through me.

"That's right, my sweet. Come for me," he urged.

My fingers bit into his ass as I pulled him closer, demanding every inch of his sex. "More."

Cris moaned and nipped my earlobe. "Careful. I'll be spent too soon."

"I don't care. I need you."

"Do you?" He sucked the lobe into his mouth, and I whimpered, unable to think, until he prompted me with another question. "Do you want me to fuck you hard until I come inside you?"

"Yes!" I nearly shouted the word as lust and need raged through me. "Please, Cris."

He growled as he rolled me to my hands and knees, pinned me to the bed and pounded me as requested. His fingers bruised my hips and I screamed into the pillow as sensation overwhelmed me—too much. The angle combined with his hard length and girth stretched me to my limits, each thrust skirting the edge between pleasure and pain.

Dear God. What happened if you fainted in a dream? Did you wake up? Fall *Inception*-style into a deeper dream? If I passed out during a sex dream with Cris would I wake in an even steamier scenario? I fisted my hands into the bedcovers and held on, my body on fire with sensation. Cris gasped, his breathing ragged. As he rode me he whispered all the things he wanted to do to me, the positions he wanted to take me in, and the ways he wanted me to beg.

"Please," I said. The word was a desperate prayer. "Please."

Cris gripped a handful of my hair, twisted it in his fist and yanked me back against him. I whimpered in surprise, but the shock was forgotten as he came inside me. He grabbed my breasts and pinched my nipples as my orgasm followed his, the aftershock to his earthquake. His cock continued to grind into me even as it softened, and his hands roamed my body, claiming every inch of me as his.

"You are amazing," he purred. "I've never met a woman like you. So sensual and strong."

*Best. Dream. Ever.* I smiled, boneless with pleasure, putty in his hands. Cris withdrew and laid me back upon the bed. He covered me in kisses as I drifted back down to earth—not the sweet kisses we'd shared in the gazebo, but hungry, bruising kisses that were as much possession as they were postcoital cuddling. Marking his territory.

"My sweet Nati. I could spend an eternity inside you and still not be sated."

I shuddered—it sounded even sexier in Spanish. Every woman should have dream sex this good.

I grinned lazily. "We'd never get any rest."

"Ah, so you would rather dream of someone else, then?" he asked, a teasing note in his voice. "I can leave you in peace. Perhaps you could count sheep instead."

"Don't you dare. You're all mine until morning."

"Yes, Nati. All yours. Forever. Tell me what you want. You have heard my desires of you. Tell me your desires of me."

"Can't you read my mind?"

He chuckled. "Perhaps, but it is so much more satisfying to hear you speak your desires out loud. Even when your accent is odd." He brushed a playful kiss atop the tip of my nose, and I giggled.

"You're the one with the odd accent." I pondered my answer as he moved to my breasts and distracted me. His lips should come with a warning label. His tongue circled my nipple, and I stroked his hair as I arched and wantonly thrust my girls toward his mouth. "I like it when you take what you want. You're forceful, but not selfish. I've been with too many men who don't know that a girl is faking because they've never given a woman a real orgasm."

"Faking?" His tone was shocked. "Surely you would not do such a thing."

"Not with you. I get wet just looking at you." I licked my lips and sighed happily. "I'm sure you've noticed."

"Hmm. Perhaps I should check to be certain..." Cris trailed kisses down my torso to my sex, and then all was pleasure until morning.

# CHAPTER TEN

I slept indecently late and woke slowly, tangled in my bedsheets and surrounded by the fading scent of great sex. I stumbled into the shower and stood under the spray until I could think coherently. I felt amazing—exhausted, but amazing. Who knew that dream sex could be so draining? Then again I'd never had dream sex this awesome and vivid before. Must be something in the water.

I wiped steam from the bathroom mirror and blinked at my reflection. Whoa. I'd really done a number on myself, even more than the first time. I frowned as I examined bite marks on my breasts and throat. They had to be souvenirs of my romp in the gazebo, but I didn't remember seeing them before I went to bed, and they looked fresh... Had Cris actually snuck into my bedroom last night, and if so, was it on film? I didn't want to explain that to the team. And it would violate the agreement, but he'd pointed that one out himself. I couldn't see him breaking the rule he'd reminded me of.

Wrapped in a towel, I returned to the bedroom and discovered that the door was locked and the chair still blocked it. Huh. So the marks had to be from the gazebo then. I approached the bed and turned down the sheets. A few faded wet spots were visible, but that wasn't unusual for me, especially when I had multiple orgasms. Yet the faint scent of roses and male lingered as well, and that made no sense.

I dressed quickly and ran a brush through my hair, then picked up my cell and called Piper direct. She answered on the fourth ring. "Do you have any idea what time it is here?"

"Honestly, no, but this is important. You're the only one I can talk to about it."

"Oh? Trouble in paradise with sexy Spanish guy?"

"Something like that. It's...well, hell, I guess it's paranormal, because it's definitely not normal."

"You have my full attention. Spill."

I explained how I'd jumped Cris in the gazebo, and how I'd had the two very vivid sex dreams.

"Wait," she said, "The first dream was the night your door opened and shut?"

"Yeah, I guess it was."

"And the second dream was last night?"

"Yes. Why?"

"Your bedroom door didn't open, but the door to the cellar did. It opened...oh, shit. It opened after you went to bed and closed just before sunrise."

"Okay. So?"

"I think...it's possible that the shadow man is an incubus."

"A what?"

"A demon who feeds on sex. He's pretending to be Cris in your dreams to gain your trust, using your attraction to lure you in."

"To what end?" I licked my lips, my mouth suddenly as dry as the Sahara.

"To drain your energy. Eventually..."

"What?" My voice jumped a stressed octave.

"The myths say that an incubus—or the female counterpart, a succubus—would fuck people to death."

"You're joking, right? I'm being punked."

"This is serious, Nati. You trust me, right?"

Shit. I did trust Piper. She was a history buff, like me, and I considered her a friend. We'd spent many a lunch hour discussing the history of California and the American Southwest.

"Yes. What should I do?"

"Right now, go have breakfast. I'll do some research and see what I can turn up."

"Don't tell the guys. They'll want to set up some kind of kinky experiment and I am so not doing that."

"Agreed. This is just between us for now."

I hung up and did as instructed. Cris was in the kitchen fixing lunch, and I grabbed his hand and pulled him outside. When I was sure we were out of camera and microphone range I threw my arms around him and held him tight.

"What's wrong?" There was concern in his voice, and he stroked my hair. "You look frightened."

"I am. I need to show you something."

"Oh?"

"Can we go to the gazebo?"

"Of course." Cris took my hand and held it tight, his grip comforting as he led me across the grounds to the rose garden. The farther from the house we walked, the better—and more foolish—I felt.

He took a seat on the couch and patted the cushion beside him. "What is wrong? You are worrying me."

I pulled my T-shirt off and pointed to the new bite marks on my breasts. "I woke up with these this morning. I didn't have them when I went to bed last night."

Cris's brow furrowed as he examined the marks. "I was perhaps too rough with you."

"That's what I thought at first too, but these are you." I pointed to marks I knew he had left. "These are fresher, and I know I didn't bite myself. So who did? My room was locked and the door was blocked by a chair. The camera on it didn't catch anyone going in or out of my room."

"That is strange. Is there anything else that could have bruised you during the night? Perhaps something in your bed? A hair comb?"

I smiled. I admired that he was so reasonable. His explanation made more sense than Piper's did, but the sick feeling in my stomach wasn't alleviated. I began to put my shirt back on, but he touched my hand to stop me.

"Must you? I am enjoying the view." Cris grinned, and I laughed. "There is one way to be certain that I left those marks and they were only late to surface."

"How?"

"To see if my mouth matches the marks. Like in a crime show, yes?" He waggled his eyebrows, and I laughed again. "Or like Cinderella's glass slipper."

"So if your mouth fits, then we live happily ever after?" I meant it as a joke, but a traitorous part of my heart lifted at the idea. An estate in Spain would be a lovely place to return to after my adventures.

"Or we get naked. Whatever happens first." Cris drew me atop his lap, and I released a shaky breath. He rubbed my arms. "You're trembling. What frightens you so?"

"Piper thinks..." I sighed. "This sounds crazy, but everything's been insane since I got here. There's something wrong with this country. I've been to dozens for locations for the show. I've trudged across muddy battlegrounds, walked through asbestos-ridden abandoned asylums, and stayed the night in haunted hotel rooms. I even stayed in the room that inspired Stephen King to write *The Shining*. And I never once experienced anything supernatural or paranormal. Not once! But one night here and it's all disembodied voices and horny shadow men."

"Perhaps it is you who are different, and not the location," he suggested.

My thought process ground to a halt. "Me?"

"By connecting with your ancestor. This place is personal to you, as I assume no other place has been."

"Well...that's true. But this place is even more personal to you. How long have you been the caretaker here?"

The corner of his mouth twitched in a faint life. "All my life. Or at least it feels that way. Some days it feels like forever."

"Then why—?" I choked back the urge to ask why he couldn't inherit the manor when Diego died. It wasn't my business. Besides, I didn't know anything about Spanish inheritance laws. Maybe it was a weird legal issue. "I thought you didn't believe in ghosts, either."

"These past few days have taught me to keep an open mind. I think perhaps there are more things in Heaven and Earth than are dreamt of in your philosophy." Cris grinned, and I was pretty sure my panties combusted. The sexy Spaniard had just quoted Shakespeare. I cleared my throat to fight the sudden urge to go down on Cris.

"But demons? Really? Piper thinks that the shadow demon has been feeding off of me. Sexually. And he's been pretending to be you to use my attraction to you."

"Should I be jealous?"

I whapped his shoulder. "This is serious."

"I know. You're tired and upset. It is understandable. But the simplest explanation is often the correct one, and the simplest explanation here is that I bruised you during our lovemaking."

"Lovemaking," I repeated, savoring the word. Cris pressed his mouth against my breast.

"A perfect fit," he murmured against the skin.

I sighed, flooded with relief. "Thank God."

Cris cupped my cheek and gazed into my eyes. "Nati, I swear to you that you are safe here. Nothing in Mendoza Manor will harm you."

I swallowed the reply that something had hurt Angela. "You can't promise that. You're not here when I'm stumbling around in the dark, poking the paranormal with electronic sticks."

"But I know this house. Only Diego knows this place as well as I do, and I am certain that there is nothing contained within its walls that can harm you. Perhaps there are spirits here, but if so, then I'm sure that they aren't evil. Sad, more likely. This is the house of weeping shadows, not violent ones."

"What should I do?" I asked.

"What would make you feel better?"

"Let me make love to you. Here, in the sunlight. I need light and life right now."

"Your wish is my command, Doña Natividad."

I took his face in my hands and kissed him. His expression was soft, sincere. Cris was worried about me, and I wasn't used to seeing that kind of concern in anyone outside of my family. He cared, and that was almost as scary as the haunted manor.

"What do you want, Cris?" I asked. "I feel like I'm taking advantage of you. Invading your space, monopolizing your time, using you for sex."

"You aren't using me. I'm an eager participant." He smiled, teasing. "I am glad that you are here. I haven't felt like this in a long time. Too long."

Agreed. Though the argument could be made that I'd never felt like this before—looking into Cris's eyes made my heart flutter in ways that would send me running for the hills if I wasn't contractually obligated to stay put.

I glanced at the chaise lounge and then studied Cris thoughtfully. "I want you naked and stretched out there, so I can have my wicked way with you."

"Of course."

I rose and stood back. Cris did as ordered, stripping his clothing and letting me enjoy the view. He lay back and I licked my lips. His sex was semi-erect, and I decided to start there. I knelt beside him and took him into my mouth. Because he wasn't hard yet he fit easily, and I savored the opportunity to tease him into a full erection.

"Nati." His hands flexed as he fought the urge to touch me.

"Touch me," I encouraged him.

Cris stroked my hair as I sucked him hard, and then I drew

away. I removed the rest of my clothing and straddled him, impaling my sex upon his cock. I shivered as I drank in the view of him stretched beneath me. His hands rested on my hips, and I traced the contours of his chest as I rocked atop him.

The sunlight shone upon us, and I marveled at the sight of our joined bodies. His tawny skin was a shade darker than mine, and I smiled at the lines of his farmer's tan. I admired that they showed that his tan was born of time spent outdoors and not from a tanning booth.

He moaned, his hips tilting to plunge himself deeper. "My God, Nati. You feel like Heaven."

"So do you." I leaned back and gripped my ankles, my body arched into a bow. I cried out in ecstasy at the feeling of his cock deep inside me, and I began to ride him. "Touch me," I repeated. This time it was an order, not a suggestion. Cris stroked my clit and brought me to a screaming orgasm.

He fought following me with a climax of his own, his breathing rough and ragged as he struggled for control. "Again, Nati. I want you to come again before I do."

I grinned. "That's very generous of you." I straightened, and then dipped forward to kiss him. My breasts brushed his chest and he ran his hands up my back.

"You look like a goddess," he said. "A goddess of the hunt. An Amazon, wild and untamed."

"You have a gifted way with words."

"I am merely inspired by your beauty."

Dear God. I descended upon him with ravenous kisses and drank in his passion, the warm afternoon sunlight, and the scent of the last of the summer roses. Nothing compared to this. His hands tangled in my hair as I writhed, and he murmured more poetic endearments against my lips. I cried out as I came, and he quickly followed, filling me with his hot seed.

I collapsed, and he held me close. "You're safe here, Nati. Nothing will hurt you, I swear it."

*Except for you.* I had an aching suspicion that my heart would end up hurt by the end of this adventure, and there was nothing I could do to stop it. Affairs with gods never ended well for the mere mortal involved.

~

"I'm not sure how I feel about investigating tonight," I said to Piper. Cris squeezed my hand reassuringly. We sat side by side—fully clothed—in the gazebo and spoke to Piper together on speaker phone.

"I know. I'm not sure how to explain it to the team," she replied.

"I don't believe you're in danger," Cris said. "I'm sure there is no sex-crazed demon roaming the halls at night. Diego would have said something."

"He wouldn't know," Piper argued. "Incubi attack women."

"Do they attack homosexual men?" Cris asked.

"I...have no idea. Why?"

"Because then Diego would know. He is only attracted to men. His partner passed away three years ago."

Oh. I was curious about what life was like for a gay man in Spain, but probably not brave enough to ask Diego when he returned. His personal life was none of my business.

Piper's long sigh hissed over the speakers. "We need more information. More data."

"So I need to investigate, is what you're saying," I said.

"Perhaps there is a simple solution to avoiding this shadow man of yours," Cris said. "Leave the lights on."

"Will that work?" I asked Piper.

"Maybe? There's some sense to it, I guess. If it's a shadow creature, then don't give it anywhere to hide. Unless it works like a weeping angel, then you'll be fucked if you blink. Literally fucked."

"Not helping, nerd."

"It's geek, not nerd, get it right," Piper corrected. "In the meantime I'm trying to get in contact with the demonologist our

Illinois team works with. She's the best in the business, but apparently she's off on her honeymoon right now and she's not answering her email. I'll keep trying. Even our b-team demonologists aren't answering our calls. It's weird."

"Right. I'll Skype you in a bit." I ended the call and rested my head on Cris's shoulder. "I have a bad feeling about this."

He kissed my forehead. "Everything will work out all right. Trust me."

"I'd feel better if you were here with me tonight."

"I will be with you in spirit, but...hmm, let's see." He unhooked the key ring attached to his belt, and then he removed a saint's medal and pressed it into my palm. "Saint Jerome. Perhaps not entirely applicable to this situation, but any protection will help."

"Jerome is patron saint of...?" I struggled to remember. I'd repressed much of my Catholic education, and they had an abundance of saints.

"Librarians."

"Why Jerome? I would've thought you'd have a Saint Christopher medal, since he's your namesake."

Cris shrugged. "I like books. The manor has a magnificent library, as you have noticed."

"I've had impure thoughts about that desk." I grinned. "And I was reading a copy of *Don Quixote*. I like ebooks because they're easier to travel with, but there's something about being able to turn the pages of an old book. It's visceral. Like being able to touch the hand of everyone who has turned the pages before you."

Cris kissed my fingers. "You have a poetic soul, Doña Natividad."

"My dad says I have an old soul. That's why I was drawn to study history. Too much time getting lost in studying the past instead of paying attention to what's going on around me in the present."

"If you're such a fan of the past, why don't you believe in the supernatural?" He turned my hand over and softly kissed the center of my palm. "Before the age of reason, everyone believed in spirits and magic."

"History is one thing. Fairy tales are another. History is made by people of action, not by wishes and magic spells. No amount of praying can change anything, other than give you bad knees. If you want something done, you need to do it yourself."

"A perfectly practical outlook for a woman named after the nativity."

I laughed. "Well, I didn't get to name myself, now did I?"

"You never wished for a fairy tale? Never wanted to be a princess? Or to marry a handsome prince?"

"Nah. Princes are charming but not sincere. And what would I do as a princess? Swan around a castle in a fancy dress while waiting for some man to save me? I'm too active for that. I'd rather be the hero, not the damsel."

Cris smiled, though the expression was strained. "I see. Would you rescue me?"

"Sure. Do you need rescuing?"

The smile faded as Cris sighed and rose. He crossed to the gazebo's edge and leaned against the rail, gazing at the garden. "An escape, perhaps. I am trapped in this place. It is a paradise and a prison."

I knew that feeling. I loved my family and I'd had a happy childhood, but I'd been afraid of following in my mother's footsteps. I was terrified by the idea of moving from my parents' home into my husband's home. Our family was Mama's world—she'd never had a life of her own. Had Cris fallen into that trap? Tended to the manor and Diego instead of pursuing his own dreams?

I laid a hand on Cris's shoulder. "What will you do when Diego...?"

"I don't know." Cris grimaced and shook his head. "I hate to see him suffer. He is a good man."

"Are you two related?"

"Yes, but I cannot inherit. It is...complicated. Diego is running out of time. As am I. I don't know what will happen to me when the estate is sold."

"I'm sorry." I squeezed his shoulder, and he took my hand and kissed it.

"There is nothing to be done about it today. You will return to your globetrotting soon, so I suggest we enjoy the time we have together."

His hands slid beneath my shirt, and I knew exactly how he intended to enjoy the rest of the afternoon.

"I'm going to video chat with my family," I told Cris over dinner. "It's morning there, but I'll be investigating while they're all settling in for dinner. Would you like to meet them?"

His brow rose, then the corners of his mouth quirked in a teasing smirk. "You wish me to meet your family? That seems serious."

"They'll probably start planning the wedding because they never meet anyone I'm dating."

Cris chuckled. "I would be honored to meet your family."

"Thank you. Just be warned that they're loud. Really loud. And they have no filters. They blurt out whatever they're thinking at the moment, no matter how inappropriate it may seem."

"I will take no offense."

I set up the call in the command center. Cris sat off to the side at first, allowing me the chance to introduce him. My brother Mike was in charge of setting up the call on my family's side—I had faith in him, and I knew that my father would never have managed it. Though he liked gadgets, Dad wasn't tech savvy. The call connected and displayed my parents' living room, packed with my relatives. My nieces and nephews played on the floor in front of the TV, and my parents were smushed in the middle of the couch.

I wasn't prepared for the flood of emotion as tears sprang to my eyes. I should be there with them. I hadn't missed a Thanksgiving in years, not since I was just starting out after college and was too poor to afford the airfare.

"Auntie Nati!" my niece Kristin shouted.

"Hey guys!" I forced the words out and waved. "Wow. You need a bigger room."

My mother smacked my father's shoulder. "I have been telling him that for years! Seven children in a three-bedroom house. *¡Díos mío!*"

I laughed, though it was a watery sound. Cris reached over and handed me a box of tissues, and I smiled gratefully.

"Hello, who is that?" Maggie asked. She was heavily pregnant with her second child.

I beckoned Cris over to join me. "This is Cris. Cris, this is my family."

He performed rather well. The kids were interested in hearing about what it was like to live in Spain. Cris was likewise interested to hear more about the details of celebrating Thanksgiving, particularly when my mother retreated to the kitchen to baste the turkeys—plural. Our family was too large to dine on just one bird.

I explained a few of the finer points of paranormal investigation, and mentioned that the network was interested in me taking Piper's place for a few episodes. Really I only shared it so that they would understand the importance of why I'd stayed in Spain, but they seemed excited by the idea of me being on TV. More excited than I was, at any rate.

We chatted for about an hour, but it was almost time for Cris to leave and I needed to set up for tonight's investigation. I teared up again when I said goodbye, and I ended the call.

Cris hugged me as I sniffled. "Your family is charming."

"That's a diplomatic way of putting it. Thanks for being a good sport."

"My family was the opposite. I had one brother, and my parents were...distant. If I had the chance, I would do things differently with them. I was angry for a long time. A very long time." Cris scowled and ran a hand through his hair.

"They're all gone?" I asked, and he nodded. "I'm sorry."

"I learned to appreciate what I have. To be content, if not at peace. It was a hard lesson. Now Diego is the only family I have left, and most days we are the only ones in this house. It is too quiet, and a bit sad. This house was meant to be lived in, to shelter a family and a house full of servants—a cook, a groundskeeper, a nanny."

I swallowed the urge to assure him that the house could have all that again, because that would be a reminder that the manor was going to be sold.

"Are you truly considering being an investigator for your show?" he asked.

"I'm not sure." I grimaced as I shrugged. "It might help my career, but it could hurt my academic reputation. I'm not interested in being famous, even D-list famous, but it's better money. I should start setting up."

"Of course."

Cris kissed me gently, and I sat alone in the empty dining room and stared down the row of vacant chairs. This room could actually house my enormous family, and we wouldn't even need to set up card tables for the kids.

Daydreaming of turkey and cranberry sauce, I rose and got to work.

## CHAPTER ELEVEN

"We want to investigate the room with the door that opened and closed last night, and the cellar."

I shook my head at John. "Not the cellar."

"You're going to need to go in there sooner or later," he replied.

"Then we'll go with later. We can start with the room, though. Which one was it?" I asked.

The room in question was a guest parlor/sitting room that was the picture of harmlessness. I couldn't imagine what a wandering spirit would want with the room enough to open the door on film, or digital film as the case might be. It was dusty—Cris mentioned that a cleaning service came in once a month to mop, dust, vacuum and launder bedding and curtains, but it was a lot of rooms to cover. I could see how the manor had needed a full-time staff in the past. The task of washing the windows alone would send me screaming.

"It's pretty boring in here," I told the team. I peered at a taxidermy deer head mounted on the wall—at least I assumed it was a deer. Some weird, Spanish deer. "Maybe it's Bambi's ghost. Do you deal with animal spirits?"

"The occasional cat spirit. There aren't any cats there?" Piper asked.

"No. This is more of a hunting dog place, but they don't have any pets." I picked up an empty crystal bud vase and looked for a manufacturer's mark. I could spot Waterford crystal, but that was about it. "Should I start with an EVP session? Maybe set up the S3?"

"Let's get a baseline EMF reading for the room and do a quick sweep with the thermal camera. If there are no readings or cold spots now we'll save the EVP session for later."

"Right."

Aside from the rem-pods, I hadn't had much luck with the EMF detectors, at least not in discovering strange spikes. Cris had informed me that the manor's electrical wiring had been upgraded five years ago (to support Diego's giant TV), so everything was well shielded. The room had a baseline reading of 1.1, which was about average for the manor. I picked up the thermal and began recording.

At first glance everything looked normal—room temperature, with the windows slightly cooler than the rest of the room. Then I realized that one of the "windows" wasn't a window at all. A rectangular patch of wall between the fireplace and the exterior wall was cooler like the windows.

"Huh. That's weird. Why is this section colder?" I asked.

"Insulation problem?" John guessed. "Go closer."

I set the camera down and turned the screen toward me so I could watch myself moving. I felt along the wall—wood paneling, very 70s rec room chic. The difference in temperature was obvious to the palms of my hands, and I felt the perimeter of the cold area.

"This isn't supernatural, right? Not normal, but not mystical?" I asked the team over my headset.

"Right."

"I wonder if it's a secret passage, like in *Clue*."

"It's possible," John said.

I snorted. "Get out. Why would they need a secret passage?"

"The Inquisition. War. Spain has a long, bloody past. Sometimes you need an escape route."

Kenji muttered something that sounded suspiciously like, "No one expects the Spanish Inquisition!"

I rolled my eyes and chewed my bottom lip. An old servants' passageway made more sense, something that was boarded up during a remodel. I channeled my inner Nancy Drew and pondered how one would open such a thing. In movies there was always a book to pull or a button to press, but that wasn't practical. The décor would need to change with the times, and old lamps and books would look blatantly out of place. Something simple, then.

"'Speak friend and enter,'" Kenji said.

I smirked. "What's the elvish word for friend?"

"Mellon."

"Seriously?" I was impressed by Kenji's level of dorkdom. "Never mind. I was thinking of just pushing real hard. I mean, it can't swing out, because there'd be wear marks on the floor."

"Try it," John suggested.

"Okay. Assuming that there's a hinge, and that the hinge would be closest to the door and the fireplace, then I should push...here."

I placed my palms against the spot in question and shoved. I thought I felt a bit of give, so I set my shoulder against it and pushed. The wall moved soundlessly—I was expecting a horror-movie creak, and the lack of noise left me unprepared. I stumbled through the open space and fell face-first with a clumsy *oof*!

The team shouted a flurry of "Are you all right?"s in my ear, and I groaned as I rolled to my butt. The secret door shut and plunged me into complete darkness. I yelped as my pulse spiked—no lights meant no safety from shadow people. I struggled to catch my breath and remain calm.

"I'm okay, guys," I said. "But I might be stuck. Lemme get my flashlight."

"We can't see you now, Nati. You're off camera," John said.

"I can't see me because it's dark." I rummaged in my messenger bag—I really hoped that I didn't break anything expensive when I fell—and finally grabbed the flashlight.

The shaky halo of LED light didn't reveal much. It was a sliver of safety in the smothering darkness. I swallowed a nervous giggle. I'd been stumbling around in the dark since I got here, but a light switch was always a few feet away. The fact that I could slap the lights on and banish the boogeyman had been comforting, but there was no such comfort here. The darkness was thick and stale, like fog pressing against my skin.

"I'm in...a hallway, I think," I said. "It's really narrow. It might've been made for servants, like those little cramped staircases in English manors."

"No elves?" Kenji asked.

I laughed, but the sound was high and thin. "No elves."

I ran the light over the secret door to find a way back into the room, but there was no knob, no handle—no way to open it from this side.

*Don't panic*. I squeezed my eyes shut and focused on several meditative breaths. I was okay. I could do this. Brave and clever, right? I opened my eyes and rolled my shoulders.

"I guess I'm going to see where this leads. I'll narrate for now."

I started down the hallway. There were no cobwebs or dust bunnies so someone must be maintaining it. Did Cris know about it? I'd never thought to ask if the manor had secret passageways, and he'd probably never thought I'd need to know about them.

"I see stairs going up and down." Presumably the stairs up led to the fourth floor.

"Go down," John said. I heard snickering in the background, followed by a disappointed sigh. "Really, guys? Are you twelve?"

I smiled as the banter eased some of my fear. "Yeah, they are. I'm going down the stairs."

I started down, slow and steady, one step at a time. The soles of my sneakers were quiet, but several wooden steps groaned ominously beneath my weight. Visions of breaking my leg as it plunged through rotten wood danced in my head, and I swallowed hard. Being locked in my room until Cris could rescue me had been easy, but waiting until his arrival while I was trapped, broken and bleeding would be hell.

Frowning, I paused at the second floor landing. Did I hear footsteps behind me? Or was that an echo in the stairwell? The acoustics had to be all kinds of messed up in here, but I wasn't making that much noise. I swiped the light over the stairs behind me but saw nothing.

"I'm going to take some EMF readings," I said.

The team didn't reply—to me, at least. I could hear them mumbling in the background, probably stunned by my initiative. I pulled the gadget from my bag and shined the flashlight's beam on the meter's readout. It was a little higher here, but nothing crazy. No spikes meant no paranormal activity, so I was safe. I read the number to the team and started down the stairs again.

I paused again at the first floor, and this time I was sure that I heard creaking wood behind me. My heart pounded as adrenaline spiked through my veins, and my hand shook as I slowly held the EMF meter in the direction of the sound.

"Two point three," I read. "Two point four." The numbers kept climbing, and I licked my dry lips. It stopped and stayed steady at a six, and I cleared my throat. "Guys? What do I do?"

Silence.

"Guys?" I prompted as my voice jumped an octave. "Little help here."

Static hissed until the earpiece let out a high-pitched electronic squeal. I cursed and pulled it off before I burst an eardrum, and the plastic gizmo slipped through my fingers and bounced down the stairs. I hurried after and found it all the way at the bottom, shattered into several sharp pieces.

"Damn it." I was alone in the dark—at least I hoped I was alone. I checked the EMF gauge again and saw that the number had returned to normal, but I also realized that I was in the basement. I could go to an upstairs floor and look for a way out, or I could start looking here. Because the cellar door had opened the same night, there was likely a connection between the secret door I'd gone through and the cellar. I just needed to stumble around the cellar with only a flashlight.

Right. No problem.

I squared my shoulders, set my jaw and started forward. The circle of light from my flashlight shook as my hand trembled, but I kept on resolutely. My heart pounded and my throat constricted until it was hard to breathe. I brushed my thumb over the lump of the St. Jerome medal in the pocket of my jeans.

"Nothing here will hurt me," I whispered, as though trying to convince myself.

I turned a tight corner and paused. A sliver of warm yellow light shone across the floor, peeking from beneath a closed door. None of the lights were on in the house except for in the command center, so I knew it wasn't the kitchen. I spotted a brass doorknob, and I reached out and turned it.

The door opened into a bedroom with a warm fire crackling in the hearth. The room was lit by candles; the buttery glow was softer than the incandescent bulbs I was used to. The air smelled of wax, smoke, and faded roses. I froze—what the actual fuck? I was alone in the house, so who the hell started the fire and lit the candles? A pyromaniac ghost? I swallowed hard and forced myself to resume breathing. There had to be a reasonable explanation. Maybe I'd stumbled on Cris's secret caretaker man cave, and he'd forgotten to blow out the candles before he left.

A few centuries of knickknacks filled shelves and crowded tabletops—a bronze sextant, a collection of blown-glass chemists' bottles, a menagerie of carved animal figurines in a variety of materials, including an elephant I was sure was ivory. Poor bastard. Above the mantle a portrait of a young dark-haired woman smiled enigmatically. I probably wouldn't have the energy to smile if I was weighed down by that much clothing. It was a lot of fabric, like a bridesmaid dress from hell.

"Nati."

I whirled as the sound of my name, but I didn't see anyone else in the room. The door shut behind me. Shit. Was I trapped?

"Hello?" My voice quavered on the word. "Cris?"

"Yes, my sweet. Who else would it be?" He chuckled, and the

sound inspired a rush of heat in my womb. Dear God. How could he make a laugh sound like phone sex?

"Who else indeed?" I murmured. My grip tightened on the flashlight. In an emergency it would work as a makeshift club. "Where are you?"

"Here, of course." I heard a rustle of cloth, and I turned toward the bed. The heavy curtains were drawn around it, but I spied a flicker of movement within. "Care to join me?"

"No, thank you. I'm fine out here," I said. He chuckled again and my nipples tightened.

"But you will feel so much better when you join me. I have missed you."

"You just saw me," I retorted. Or at least my Cris had. The lusty sex demon hadn't had the pleasure of my company since last night.

"Every moment away from you is a tragedy, my sweet."

"Right. How about you show me how to get back upstairs? Please?"

The candles around me winked out one by one, until only my flashlight and the fire in the hearth remained. Candle smoke stung my eyes, and I backed toward the door I'd entered through. I turned to open it and smacked into a naked chest. I yelped as the flashlight was knocked from my hand and rolled away under a book case.

"Shh, Nati. You know that I would never hurt you."

Wide-eyed, I stared at a very naked and very happy to see me Cris. But it wasn't Cris, not entirely. His features were the same, but from head to toe he was dark, as though covered in soot—soot that moved and swirled on his skin like a living sandstorm.

*Shadow.* He was made of shadow. I screamed and stumbled back, crashing into a table.

"Nati, please. Listen to me—"

Ignoring him, I dove after the flashlight. I scrabbled under the bookcase like a dog after a bone that had rolled under a radiator. Light. I needed light to make him go away.

"I won't hurt you. I won't touch you without your consent." He purred *consent* as though the word was naughty.

"I'm not consenting! Get the hell away from me and leave me alone." Dust bunnies. So many damn dust bunnies that my fingers turned gray. I cursed and pressed my face against the floor as I peered for a glimpse of the flashlight's matte black handle. Why the hell hadn't they made it in neon green? Or reflective yellow, like lane lines on the highway?

"I can't. I need your help. Please."

Ayúdame. Por favor.

I paused and turned my head slightly, just enough to peer at his bare feet. "Help to do what?"

"To end the curse that binds me."

I gnawed on my bottom lip until I tasted blood—I was going to need some serious moisturizer at the rate I was damaging my skin—and then I slowly pushed to my knees. I unzipped my hoodie and tossed it in his direction. "If you want to talk, tie that around your waist. I can't deal with your flagpole saluting me."

He chuckled, and I stifled a moan as the erotic sound rumbled through my body as if his smiling mouth was pressed against my sex. He tied the pink hoodie around his waist as ordered, and the ridiculousness of it eased some of my fear. Demons didn't look good in pink.

I rose and crossed my arms. "What do you want?"

"My freedom, and only you can grant it."

I snorted, suspicious. "Speak plainly or I start screaming and throwing things. Breakable things. *Expensive* things."

The demon held his hands up—no claws or hooves. Shouldn't a demon have horns and a tail? It looked exactly like Cris, just with the shadowy special effect. No amount of makeup artistry could accomplish the movement across his skin, so I was confident that the network wasn't tormenting me. I'd fallen down the rabbit hole and entered Spanish Wonderland.

"It isn't a plain issue, but I will do my best. I was born Don Cristóbal Mendoza Ríos."

"You're the Cristóbal who married Angela?"

"The same," he confirmed. "I was no mere mortal man, but a librarian in service to the Order of Saint Jerome. The Order is tasked with keeping the history of magic and magicians."

"Magic?" I repeated skeptically. "Real magic?"

He nodded, and the candles in the room flared to life again. As the candles glowed, Cris's form faded in the light, as though caught in the middle of being beamed away by Scotty. Curious, I stepped forward and poked his forearm with my index finger. The skin was warm—feverishly hot—and shadows gathered where I touched him. I felt lightheaded, but I fought the sensation back.

"What happened to you?"

"I was a fool." The candles winked out again, and as his face solidified I spotted a rueful smile. "I was arrogant, and in my arrogance I seduced and abandoned a woman by the name of Isabel Vásquez. She was a summoner—a magician who deals in demons—and I made a powerful enemy in her when I ended our affair. But I had fallen in love with Angela."

Cris turned and gazed mournfully at the portrait. "Angela was a beautiful, virtuous woman. Sweet, innocent and giving. She had a voice like an angel, like you. But, also like you, she had no magic or knowledge of magicians. I didn't care. I was obsessed with her. I wanted her as my bride."

"And Isabel didn't take this well?"

"No. She summoned a powerful demon to murder Angela, and when I realized what had happened I confronted her. Isabel laughed—laughed! She said since I had behaved like a lustful beast, then I would spend eternity as one. She cursed me into this form. By day I am a man, as you have seen. But when the sun sets I become this." He waved a hand over his body. "A creature of darkness who lives only to fuck."

Cris held his face in his hands, and I stuck my hands in my jeans pockets to resist the urge to comfort him. "So you've been stuck here ever since?"

"Yes."

"How do I figure into this?"

"You were the first woman who was not afraid of me. I am drawn to the women who visit the manor. Not to my kin or their wives, nor to young girls. Over the years..." Cris shook his head and walked away. The sight of my hoodie covering him was only more ridiculous from behind, but his ass was still magnificent despite being covered in shadow stuff and framed with the tied sleeves forming an awkward bow.

"I get it. You traumatized women. Except me, because I'm all sexually liberated." I smiled dryly.

"You were miraculous. I've never met a woman as confident in her desire are you are. Every woman should be so secure in her passion."

"Agreed. So...you want to continue having sex with me? I don't see how that solves your problem."

"You are a member of Angela's family. I believe you can break the curse and restore my humanity. You can save me."

No pressure there. My pulse raced as I fought down a severe panic attack. Sure, I'd said I wanted to be a heroine, but damn. "How? I don't know a thing about magic."

"I am not certain yet, but you give me hope, and hope is a gift I have not received in centuries."

I swallowed hard as tears stung my eyes. It was a terrible story of evil and death, but he was a demon. Demons lied. "How do I know you're telling the truth?"

"You have my medal in your pocket."

"What?"

He gestured toward my jeans. "My St. Jerome medal is in your pocket. I gave it to you so that you would feel safe. And you are safe, my Nati. Nothing in this house will harm you. Not even myself, though it is difficult..."

"You want to hurt me?" I asked, my voice jumping an octave.

Cris turned toward me, his gaze heavy and searing. "I want to bury my cock inside of you. Your mouth, your sex, your ass. I want you covered in my seed, screaming my name as you find release after release. I want you to ride me as you did in the gazebo. You were stunning in the sunlight, arched above me like a pagan goddess." He stepped forward, then stopped and clenched his hands into fists. "But I want you to be willing. It is my great shame that my curse has driven me to force myself on unwilling women, sneaking into their bed to steal their passion like a thief. I cannot do that to you. I never want to do that again. I will not be a monster even one moment longer."

"Why did you do it?" I asked. "Because of the curse?"

"Yes. I am...not quite a full incubus. They feed from sexual desire, and drain a woman's mortality while they feed, even unto death. I have the compulsion to feed, but my victims are unharmed. Most women think it only a dream, as you did."

Nodding, I reached into my pocket and rubbed the medal between my thumb and forefinger, finding strength in the symbol. "I need to get back upstairs. The team is probably freaking out."

"Of course. I...would you...?" He sighed, frustration shuddering through him down to his toes. "I have a landline down here. You could call, reassure them. Tell them that you are unable to leave the cellar until I can rescue you in the morning."

"So I can play hooky down here and let you ravish me?" I replied. "Are you crazy? Why should I trust you? You lied to me. You've been lying from the start. You chased me around the house like some B horror movie monster and nearly gave me a heart attack."

"Would you have listened to the truth? You were a skeptic with no reason to believe me. You needed to experience the supernatural for yourself." Cris's chin rose a stubborn fraction and my temper flared.

"I was honest with you. I trusted you. I told you things I never talk about with anyone, and you lied to me. What else are you hiding?"

He opened and shut his mouth as his brow furrowed.

"See? You're still not being honest with me." I pointed an angry finger in his direction. Cris took a step toward me and I grabbed the nearest bauble. He froze as I wound up to hurl it like a fastball. "Spill, Señor Sombra. Who were the demons who invaded the house?"

"You saw that?" He seemed taken aback by the idea.

"Yeah, we saw that. Let me guess. You turned the cameras off."

"I did. I thought it best that your team not record what happened."

"What did happen?"

He sighed and grimaced. "They were Isabel's minions. They have been attacking the wards for days."

"Wards?"

"A magical barrier meant to protect things within it. That is how I first knew you were at Angela's grave. I felt you breach the ward. I thought you were a magician, perhaps one under Isabel's sway."

"She's still alive? Is that normal?"

"She is a demon now, or at least she is more demon than magician at this point."

I scowled and set the trinket back in its spot. No amount of breaking things would make me feel better. "You should have been honest with me."

"I am being honest with you now. I have faith in you, Natividad. You are my only chance at redemption. You must decide if you have faith in me."

Faith. I didn't do well with faith, so I tried to organize the facts I had. Cris hadn't hurt me. I'd been scared by some of the paranormal shenanigans, but not harmed. I felt fine—good even. Cris could've left more than a few love bites if he'd had a mind to hurt me. Hell, he'd had ample opportunities to snap my neck or choke me to death. I wasn't sure about any of this, but my gut told me that he wasn't evil.

I am tied to this land. Nowhere is pleasing to me.

Cris was living my nightmare, multiplied by a thousand—he was trapped in a life he didn't want with no chance of escape. He was giving me a chance to be a heroine. What kind of knight in shining armor would I be if I let my damsel down? I couldn't abandon him now. I'd see this through.

"Give me the landline."

Cris grinned, his teeth shockingly white against his shadowy countenance. He led me to a side table and uncovered an old touchtone phone complete with a curling cord and a receiver the size of a shoe. Oh man. I couldn't remember the last time I used one of those. The 90s?

Piper answered her cell on the second ring.

"Hey, it's Nati," I told her. "I'm okay, but I'm stuck in the cellar."

"Oh my God! You scared the crap out of us. What happened?"

"The earpiece went all staticky, and I dropped it. It broke. I followed the stairs into the basement, and now I'm stuck in a workshop. I think I may do some woodworking. Maybe make a bookend or something."

"You can't get out?" she asked.

"Door is locked from the other side. I called Cris's cell first, and he said he can spring me when he gets here in the morning. For now I'm going to make like a Girl Scout and curl up in this sleeping bag."

I heard John in the background. "Well if she's going to be in the cellar and she has her bag..."

"Hell no. Tell him I'm done for the night. Cris will help me poke around the secret passages in the daylight. That's as good as it gets."

"All right. I'll let him know. Hey, what happened with the EMF readings you were taking?"

"They spiked, and then they stopped. We can work on that again tomorrow too." I grimaced, because that was the only true thing I'd said since I called. It was for the best. No matter how big a ratings boost the show would get from filming a real demon, the team didn't need to know about this. Cris's life was more important.

"Right. Try to get some sleep."

"You, too. You're sleeping for two you know."

Piper laughed. "Hard to forget when she keeps kicking me in the kidneys. Nati, I'm glad you're okay."

"No more Nancy Drew for me. This stuff is all you guys. Good night, Piper." I hung up the phone—weird. So used to swiping a red button or clicking disconnect.

"Your friend is expecting?" Cris stood behind me, so close that I felt the heat of his body through my clothes.

"Yes. It's her first." I laid my palms atop the table and took a deep breath. My pulse pounded and I swallowed hard. "If I help you break your curse, what will you do?"

"Do?" Cris traced a finger beneath my ear, down the side of my neck and over my T-shirt between my shoulder blades.

"You're here because of the curse, right? Once it's gone, you could go anywhere. Do anything. What do you want to do?"

"Travel. See all the places I've only read about or watched on television. I must admit, Diego's high definition television is quite the technological marvel." Cris pressed a burning kiss against the joint of my neck and shoulder. "It has been so long since I had any hope of escape. I stopped making plans long ago. Come to bed, Natividad. I *need* you."

He growled the word like a man starving to death, and my knees wobbled. A whisper of cloth behind me heralded that Cris had removed my sweatshirt.

How insane was it that I was considering consensual demon sex? Well, semi-demon sex. But this was Cris. The real question was whether or not I trusted him enough to do this. It was sort of a sexy leap of faith.

"If I do this—if we do this—I need your word that from now on you will tell me the truth, the whole truth, and nothing but the truth. No lies of omission. No half-truths."

"You have my word."

"And if I find out that you've lied to me about anything from this point on—and I do mean anything—I'm out of here. Understood?"

"Understood."

I swallowed hard. "All right."

Cris gripped the hem of my T-shirt and pulled it over my head, then unhooked my bra and slipped the straps forward so that the garment slipped down my arms and onto the tabletop, linking my hands like lacy restraints. Cris brushed my hair aside and kissed the nape of my neck as his hands slipped around my waist to the button of my jeans.

With nimble ease he unfastened my pants and had them and my panties around my ankles. He knelt behind me to remove my shoes, pausing to bite one of the fleshy cheeks of my ass. I yelped and he chuckled, and I was suddenly naked. Cris nudged my legs further apart, and then traced the slit of my sex. I was wet already, and I shivered in anticipation.

"Lean forward, my sweet. I'm going to taste you."

I whimpered as I obeyed, resting my forehead on my folded arms. It seemed like an odd angle for a blow job, but then his tongue slipped into my channel as his fingers found my clit, and I cried out in hungry approval. Cris moaned as though savoring a fine wine.

Desire and pleasure raged through me like wildfire, consuming my ability to think and leaving only quivering submission in its wake. Cris brought me to climax and then pushed me further, enthusiastically drinking in my orgasm and the sound of my moans.

"Again," he ordered. Cris pushed two fingers inside me and stroked my G-spot as he covered my ass and the backs of my thighs with bruising love bites.

*Mine. My Nati.* Cris had claimed my body. Should I be worried about my soul? I hadn't thought about that in years. With his clever mouth and relentless fingers he worked me from one height to the next until I lost count of orgasms and my throat was raw with eager screaming. Time melted, and I was limp and boneless as he continued to take me. Finally he withdrew, but before I could catch my breath he thrust his cock inside me. Cris rode me relentlessly, driving deep into my dripping pussy. All I could do was grip the table and hold on.

After I came screaming twice, Cris grabbed my hair and hauled me back against him. “I want you in my bed,” he growled in my ear. “I want you bound and blindfolded until sunrise.”

“And then?”

“And then I will make love to you as myself, and sweetly worship every inch of you like a lord revering his lady.”

I smiled at the image, and I understood. The demon needed all the raw, raunchy sex I could give him, but the man wanted my heart. I wasn’t sure about my heart, yet, but the kink I could handle.

“Yes,” I moaned. “Please, Cris.”

He withdrew instantly, swept me into his arms and carried me to the bed. I kept my eyes closed until the silk blindfold was slipped over my head. The scent of the room became sharper with my vision removed from the equation. It smelled of sex—hot, sweaty, dripping sex tinged with the musk of aroused male, all suffused with candle smoke and faded roses. A slick, cool length of silk bound my wrists together and then stretched my arms above my head, likely tied to the headboard.

“My Nati. You are so beautiful. I have never seen anything as lovely as you in my bed.”

Cris descended upon me, ravenous, scorching my skin with kisses that claimed every inch of my body from my wrists to my toes. He stroked and pinched, bit, sucked and nibbled, pushed and pulled as I moaned in encouragement. I’d never felt so taken in my life. I belonged to this tortured, cursed man. I would never be the same.

He straddled my stomach and fucked my tits until he came, covering my chest and throat. Cris left his seed to soak into my skin as he knelt beside my head, grabbed my hair and tugged my head to the side so he could fuck my mouth. Greedily I sucked him hard again until he came down my throat.

“Mine,” he murmured.

I licked my lips and savored the taste of his climax. I enjoyed giving blow jobs as much as I enjoyed receiving them—I loved the control of teasing my partner to orgasm. Cris lay between my thighs, draped my legs over his shoulders and returned to pleasuring my sex with his lips and tongue.

"My Nati. So sweet. I could spend all night tasting you."

"No argument here," I replied.

Cris chuckled, and I came instantly. "And so responsive. I can't wait to hear you moan when I take your ass."

"You're lucky I like you. I don't usually do anal."

"You haven't had good anal sex then. It's exquisite when done right."

"Says the guy who's pitching instead of catching," I retorted. But I was willing to give him the benefit of the doubt. Maybe his sex demon powers made anal awesome instead of awkward and uncomfortable.

After that, everything became a blur of life-changing pleasure. I couldn't think straight—I could hardly form coherent words, and only managed to moan, sigh and scream my approval as Cris fulfilled every item on his naughty wish list. I was consumed by sensation, cresting ever increasing waves of erotic ecstasy. I was wanton and wicked and I loved every moment of it. Finally I reached a point of exhaustion, and I fainted—an honest-to-goodness, Victorian-heroine-with-consumption swoon. I'd never fainted before in my entire life, not even when my idiot brother Sean broke his arm in three places after jumping off the garage roof and then felt compelled to prove to his family that his broken arm could bend in any direction like Stretch Armstrong.

I woke to find my restraints removed and my blindfold gone. Cris—real Cris, not demony Cris—sat beside me, gently washing the mess of fabulous sex from my body while murmuring endearments.

"Hi," I greeted. "How are you?"

"Are you well?" Cris seemed hesitant, afraid to meet my gaze.

"Exhausted, but otherwise okay. To be perfectly honest, I seriously need to pee. Is there a washroom down here?"

"Yes, there is. I will show you." He chuckled as he helped me up, and though it was still a sexy sound it didn't have the orgasm-inducing ability of his demon self.

Apparently my legs were no longer attached to my brain, because when I tried to stand I almost faceplanted immediately. Cris saved me and kept me upright until I could figure out how walking worked.

"Holy cow. I really can't walk straight. That is actually a thing. A real thing," I babbled.

"Yes. I should have warned you that might happen."

"You've done this before? Don't answer that," I ordered. "I'm happier thinking that I'm the only one whose world you've rocked this hard."

Cris deposited me in a lovely bathroom, likely recently remodeled, and left me to take care of business. The shower had a million fancy showerheads, and I knew exactly what we were going to do after I relieved my dangerously full bladder. Demon Cris was lucky I hadn't accidentally given him a golden shower (which was something that was definitely not on my naughty checklist).

It was a masculine bathroom—no frilly details or feminine touches. I was intrigued by the shaving tools. No loud electric razor for the lord of the manor. When I was blessedly relieved I washed my hands then returned to bedroom. Cris hovered just outside the door, likely worried that I was going to go all jelly legs again and collapse. I took his hand and pulled him inside.

"Strip," I ordered. His brow rose. "We're going to shower. I'll wash your back if you wash mine."

"Are you certain—?"

"Yes. Strip. Now."

I stood next to the shower and pondered how it worked. It wasn't a cheap plastic stall like the one my parents had put in the bathroom they'd added in their basement. Expensive mosaic tile lined two walls, and glass formed the other two. Myriad nozzles jutted from the tile in all direction and at all heights.

"Whoa. It's like showering in a hurricane," I said.

Cris laughed. "Perhaps. I was intrigued by the concept of it. The jets are meant to be massaging."

"Huh. Well, there's definitely room for two."

I enjoyed the view as he twisted nozzles and the water leaped to life. He extended a hand to me and drew me into the shower as though inviting me to a waltz. I stepped close and wrapped my arms around him in a tight hug. I laid my head against his chest and snuggled, and was pleasantly surprised by how right it felt. His embrace was calming and comforting—an emotional connection instead of the overwhelming lust that had been raging through us like two hormonal teenagers each time we were together.

"I'm okay," I assured him. "You never answered my question. Are you all right?"

"I wish you did not have to see me like that," he admitted, his voice tight. "I don't want to frighten you, and I don't want you to think that sex is all I want from you. You are amazing in every way."

"Ooh, I like that. You should write my résumé."

Cris tilted my face up and studied me, his brow furrowed with concern. "You are truly fine with what occurred last night? No regrets?"

"Really fine. You can trust me, Cris. I want to help you."

"You are helping me. You are my hope, Natividad. You have brought me back to life. I was afraid... Diego is my last living heir. When he passes, the house will be sold. I don't want to spend eternity hiding in the walls by day and stalking bedrooms at night."

How awful. Cris was bound to the house, and that was something no real estate agent wanted to put on their listing.

"Well, let's hope that I can break your curse. But now we'd better hurry. The team is probably watching the cameras, waiting for you to show up and rescue me."

# CHAPTER TWELVE

We sped through the shower, barely managing to keep our roaming hands to a minimal amount of groping. Then I dressed and braided my hair—hoping that the team wouldn't notice that it was wet—while Cris left through a secret tunnel to the edge of the estate that allowed him the illusion of "arriving" each morning.

When I emerged into the kitchen I waved awkwardly at the camera. "I'm fine. I'm going to go change."

"I will fix us something for breakfast," Cris said.

"That would be lovely, thank you."

I hightailed it upstairs and froze two steps inside of my room. The bed was trashed—the mattress and pillows were ripped apart, stuffing strewn around like an exploded bag of microwave popcorn. The bed curtains were shredded as if a tiger had taken offense to them.

"Cris!" I shouted. "Cris, come here!"

I heard his bounding footsteps before he arrived. I pointed at the mess. "What the hell is this?"

He stared, and then he scowled. "Isabel's minions," he said, careful to keep his voice low. "I didn't sense them because we were preoccupied. She must know that you are here."

"Damn it. I'm going to change clothes. Don't leave."

"I swear I shall not leave your side," Cris vowed.

My stomach did a fluttery roll and I grinned. My dark knight in shadowy armor. Hmm, he was sort of Bruce Wayne-like—giant creepy house, secret identity. I dressed with record speed, and then we returned to the kitchen to fix a quick breakfast. I would've skipped it under the circumstances, but we were both in urgent need of food and caffeine after last's night marathon sex. We brought the meal to the command center.

"Are you okay?" John asked as soon as the call connected.

"Yes, I'm fine. I have a crick in my neck from sleeping on a crappy camping bed, but I'm fine. But my room looks like someone took a weedwhacker to it." Fingers crossed that their habit of just missing recording actual, full-body apparitions was still holding.

"We caught a ton of activity last night. It's crazy," John replied. "I've never seen anything like this before."

"And this activity includes an intruder?" Cris asked.

"Not a human one," Kenji said.

"Show us what you have, and then we'll show you the room," I said.

Cris shot me a dubious glance, but we continued. The team brought up the footage. Short, blurry shadows darted down the hallway, the door opened and shut, and then a chorus of bangs and growls accompanied the sound of tearing fabric.

"What's the time on this?" I asked.

"It started at three thirty-three," John said. "And that's bad. It's a sure sign of demonic activity because it mocks the holy trinity."

Cris snorted, though I didn't think the team heard his reaction. Cris and I had been well into our orgy by then, so he was right that we missed it in our distraction.

"Anything else?" I asked.

"We're still analyzing the sound. The door opens again at four." John fast-forwarded the footage to the spot in question, and the door burst open and more shadow blurs exited. "What happened to your room?"

I picked up my tablet and carried it upstairs. I showed the team the destruction, and they were appropriately disturbed.

"Is Piper there?" I asked.

"No, she went home after you called. We ordered her to get some rest and stop stressing," John explained.

Shit. I needed to ask her about that demonologist. "Okay. You guys keep analyzing. Cris and I are going to get some fresh air and come up with a battle plan for tonight."

"I will show you the other passages later," Cris spoke up. "I did not think you would need to know about them, so I did not mention them. I apologize for the oversight."

I squeezed his hand and ended the call. We picked up more coffee and a bowl of fruit and headed out to the gazebo.

"What kind of demon are Isabel's minions?" I asked after we settled in.

Cris scowled as he picked up a bright red apple. "There are many different breeds of demon, but her servants are shadow demons. They come from the shadow realm."

"Shadow realm?" I repeated. This was all too *Lord of the Rings* for me.

"There are many worlds. Magicians can access some of these worlds, such as Faerie."

My jaw dropped. "Holy shit. Faeries are real?"

"Faeries, vampires, werewolves, all sorts of myths and monsters that humanity stopped believing in. The monsters prefer it that way. It is safer. For them. Us." Cris smiled sadly and shook his head. "When I was cursed I was expelled from my order. My brethren blamed me for my condition, claiming that I deserved my curse due to my indiscretion with Isabel. Magic ran in my family, and the others of my blood were likewise rejected. Other magician families shunned us, so my kin were forced to marry those with no magic at all. Over time, their power dwindled, until it was gone.

Diego has no magic. If he did, he would not have contracted his illness. Magicians are immune to cancer."

"That's awful. I'm so sorry." I squeezed his shoulder, and he took my hand and kissed it.

"Isabel...as I said, she was a summoner. They trade pieces of their soul for favors from demons, until finally their soul is lost and they become a demon themselves. That is why Isabel is still alive."

"She's still holding a grudge after all these years?"

"Women." Cris shrugged, and I whapped him on the shoulder. He grinned and kissed my hand again. "If nothing else, it means we must be close to ending the curse. Otherwise she would not have taken note of us."

"Will her servants come back?" I asked.

"It is possible. I will protect you."

"Who's going to protect you?" I countered. "I mean, you're cursed, and you're unaging, but are you immortal? Can they kill you?"

"Perhaps. I tried to kill myself during a very dark period after my curse. I was unsuccessful. Each time I woke again as the demon at nightfall."

I frowned. "Huh. Let's avoid testing that then. We need backup."

"Indeed. I don't know what to do, other than to ask Diego to return."

"I'm going to call Piper." I picked up my cell phone. "I'll put her on speaker."

"How will that help?" Cris asked, his brow furrowed.

"Hey," Piper greeted. "Are you okay?"

"Yeah, I'm fine. I'm here with Cris. Are you okay? The boys said they sent you home."

"Yeah. Weird food cravings combined with acid reflux. I'll survive."

"Please tell me you've heard from your demonologist contact."

"Sort of. I got in touch with her assistant, Harvey. He said he'd pass the information on. Why?"

"Because it's gotten way worse." I explained about the demon party crashers who had torn up my room. "They'll be back, and we could use some help dealing with that."

"Whoa. Okay. I'll call Harvey and update him. In the meantime you need to keep all the lights on."

As if on cue a crack of thunder startled Cris and me, and we both jumped. He rose and stared out of the gazebo.

"A storm is coming," he said.

"Great. That was unnecessarily ominous. Please tell me you have a backup generator," I said to Cris.

"No."

"You do, for the cameras," Piper said. "It should be with the rest of equipment. It'd be enough to power a few lamps."

"Fire will help as well. Many of the rooms have a fireplace," Cris added.

"Is the chapel still there?" Piper asked.

"What chapel?" I asked.

"I pulled an old map of the manor," she said. "One of the outbuildings was a chapel."

"How did you find such a thing?" Cris asked.

"I accessed the online archives of the University of Barcelona. Or rather one of our European chapters did, and they sent me the info."

"Nice work," I said, impressed.

"Yes, the chapel is still there," Cris said. "Though it is in disrepair."

"But it's still consecrated ground?" Piper asked.

"To my knowledge, though that may not deter them."

I shrugged. "It's worth a shot. Okay, Piper, you call this Harvey person. We're going to prepare for the storm." I hung up and sighed. We did not need another challenge. I checked the local weather radar and winced at the angry red blob approaching our location. "This is bad. Severe storm warning bad."

"We will be all right," Cris assured me.

"I wish I had your confidence. I'm still trying to figure out where this all went weird. One minute I'm about to get on a plane back to the States, and then it's all demons and magic and the best sex ever. I'm okay with the sex part. The rest..."

Cris crossed to me and knelt at my feet. "The best sex ever, eh?"

"Definitely. Though I imagine that after a few centuries you've had time to perfect your technique."

He blushed—blushed!—and looked away. "No. Many women were afraid. Not always of me, but of embracing their own passion. Afraid that sex, even in their dreams, was a sin."

"Funny how men don't suffer from that kind of shaming," I said dryly. "Though I guess you did. Why..." I trailed off, and Cris quirked an eyebrow. "Why were you with Isabel, if you didn't love her? Not that I'm saying that sex has to come with love attached. Whatever goes on between two consenting adults is their personal business. I'm just... Well, she was obviously seriously pissed at you to do this. I can't imagine ever being mad enough at someone to curse them into demonhood."

"Ours was a tempestuous relationship. We were obsessed with each other, and I came to realize that was not healthy. Certainly not for a marriage. As much as I lusted for her, I knew that we could not live with each other, or raise a family together. We were a bonfire, and I wanted a hearth fire."

"And Angela fit the bill?"

"She was a remarkable woman. I did more than lust after her. I admired and respected her. Angela was beautiful, but also had a kind heart and a generous spirit. Everyone who encountered her adored her."

I wrinkled my nose. "She sounds like a Disney princess. Like tweeting birds and talking mice followed her around."

"Perhaps. Regardless, she deserved a much kinder fate than she met. I understand why her spirit cannot rest. I wish I could give her the peace she deserves. I'm glad that Diego devised this arrangement to aid her."

"Just her?" I asked, and he smiled. "Maybe she will rest when your curse is ended."

"I hope so."

"Okay. Enough angst. I need you to tell me everything you know about fighting shadow demons."

"Very well." Cris rose and drew me to my feet. "Come. We have much to prepare."

The approaching storm was a doozy, and the team was excited because thunderstorms are said to increase paranormal activity. But because of the impending lightning bonanza we disconnected the computers and cameras from the house's power and attached them to the generator, and that was time consuming. Though the storm had brought an early darkness we still had an hour and a half until actual sunset, so Cris used the time to give me the tour of his hidden rooms. He had his own luxury suite carefully tucked away in the cellar, safe from prying eyes.

"This is the library. My family's library, when we were still magicians. I have tended it, but I have not been able to acquire new books for over a century."

I stuffed my hands in my pockets to avoid the temptation to stroke the spines of the books. The shelves were lovingly tended, not a speck of dust or disorder in sight. "These are spell books?"

"Some are. Many are journals or historical texts. Our history is separate from that kept by voids. People devoid of magic," Cris explained before I could ask him to define the term.

"So even if I read one of these spell books, I wouldn't be able to do magic?"

"Sadly no."

"Are you sure, though?" I asked. "There are several generations between me and Angela, and my entire family on my dad's side. I'm willing to bet there's a bruja in my mother's family tree."

"Perhaps." He nodded slowly and scratched his jaw with a

pensive expression. "There is sense to that. It would explain why I felt you breach the ward, when a void would not have affected it all."

"Is there a test? Some kind of supernatural aptitude exam?"

"There are methods we can try, but each will take more time than we have at the moment."

My spirits lifted at the idea of ditching muggle-hood for magic —it would open a whole new vista of potential research. "Why is your history separate? It seems like you could do so much to help people. Why hide what you are?"

Cris sighed. "Because mankind has a long, bloody history of intolerance. In ancient times we lived side by side, but then the voids turned on magic and magicians. They drove the elves into extinction."

"Elves are real?" I asked, surprised. Kenji would be so thrilled to know that.

"Not anymore." He grimaced. "Even today there are groups who hunt magicians. It is a dangerous life. You would be safer as a void."

"You can't show me an entire library of history that I've never heard of before and then tell me I can't read it. That's the height of cruelty."

Cris drew me into his arms and affectionately kissed my forehead. "You could read them, if you stay."

"Stay?" I repeated.

"Stay here, with me. There is plenty of room in the manor, and I can provide for you."

"You mean, we could live here together after I cure you?" Was I asking a lot of questions? It felt like the room was spinning, or that the walls were closing in.

"Or if you do not cure me. You could inherit the house and fortune. Diego is prepared to name you as his sole heir."

I blinked. "Whoa. That's...a lot of responsibility. And commitment."

"You do not need to make a decision now."

"Good, because I'd need some serious time to ponder that." I nudged him away before I began to hyperventilate from a full-blown panic attack. "Show me something magic."

He cocked an eyebrow. "My cursed form was not evidence enough?"

"I want to see something different. Something fun. Shiny."

"I'm not certain that I know any shiny spells."

I placed my hands on my hips. "You have this entire library of arcane lore and not one spell that can outdo a sparkler from a package of grocery-store fireworks?"

His brow furrowed—probably trying to figure out what grocery-store fireworks were—and I sighed. "Okay. How do I fight a demon?"

"You are not to engage them."

"Are you going to tell them that? Because judging by how hard they murdered my bedding, I'm guessing that they're looking for a fight."

"True." He grimaced, and I fought the urge to kiss his pouty lips. It was ridiculous that the man looked sexy even when cranky. "Demons cannot be killed. They can only be banished back to their home realm. Any magician can banish a demon through words and physical contact."

"So...all I need to do is slap one and tell it to go to hell?"

Cris looked rather like a man who had just swallowed a bug, but he nodded. "That is not how I would have put it, but yes."

"Good. Continue the tour."

"Ah, yes." Cris sighed in relief and led me farther into the room. "Well, this is my desk. I would very much like to see you naked atop it."

"Now that is something I can agree to."

I felt like a naughty undergrad as I stripped. Cris kept his clothing on as he sat in the heavy desk chair, a throne of polished wood and aged chocolate leather that probably cost more than all the furniture in my apartment combined. He looked like a king about to pass judgment on his subjects. I licked my lips and anticipated enjoying fulfilling his royal decrees.

When I was naked, Cris ordered me to sit on the edge of the desk atop the green blotter. He slid the chair closer, picked up each of my ankles and gently set my feet atop the arm rests. My face flushed at being spread before him, my sex open like a book.

"Touch yourself," he ordered. "I want to watch you bring yourself to orgasm."

"Do you have a business suit?" I asked. Cris blinked at the non sequitur. "I have a weakness for men in suits. I get wet at the idea of you in a three piece suit. Even wetter when I imagine the fun we could have with a necktie."

He grinned. "Do you wish me to change?"

"Not now. We can try it tomorrow." I dipped my hand between my legs and stroked my clit. "I wish I had my toys. I tried bringing a vibrator on vacation once and Homeland Security rifled through my bag. Perverts."

Cris's gaze slid from my face to my sex and his focus traced a scorching path across my skin. I cupped my breast with my other hand, rolling and pinching my nipple. Shocks of pleasure jolted from my breast to my core. Cris licked his lips as his hands alighted on my feet, then slowly stroked up my legs to bracket my hips.

"You are so beautiful, Nati. Is that how you prefer to be touched? Like so?" Cris laid his fingers over mine as I hurriedly stroked my mound, teasing my clit and the wet folds at once.

"Yes. Side to side, fast and with just a bit of pressure. Too hard and I end up sore." I paused as hungry warmth coiled within me. "Touch me."

"As you wish." Cris beamed a sultry smile and pushed two fingers into my channel. I moaned as he flexed his fingers and stroked my inner walls. "Your eyes darken when you are aroused. It's quite fascinating."

I worked myself to a fast orgasm, and the walls of my sex clenched around Cris's thrusting fingers. His own eyes darkened as he slipped his fingers free and then raised them to his lips for a taste. "So sweet," he murmured. I nearly came again simply from watching him savor me. "Lay back."

I did as ordered, and Cris lowered his face to my mound. My hips bucked as his mouth did sinful, skillful things to my sex. My knuckles whitened where I gripped the edge of the desk, desperate for stability as the pleasure threatened to shatter me into orgasmic pieces. Cris was relentless, and I loved it.

Could I really stay with him? A life of awesome sex was appealing, but I couldn't spend all day, every day having sex like a nymphomaniac. At least I assumed that I couldn't. The past few days seemed to prove the contrary.

I moaned his name when I came again. Cris rose and unzipped his pants, freed his erection and sheathed his hard cock inside of me. His fingers dug into my hips as he fucked me hard and fast. Raw need clouded his expression as he groaned and panted. His hands moved to grip the undersides of my knees, pulling me even wider.

"Wait," I said. Cris ground to a halt. "I've had you hot and hard. Let's go slow. I want to watch you move."

"Like this?" He withdrew so that only his tip was still inside my sex, and then he slid in, inch by tantalizing inch.

"Yes," I gasped. "I need to see you."

Cris stretched one of my legs up his chest and kissed my ankle. I was silently impressed that I was that flexible. He caressed my calf, my thigh, then laid his hand beside our joined flesh. "Beautiful," he agreed. "I had forgotten how amazing the sight of two becoming one truly is. Your sex fits mine like a glove. As though we were made for each other."

I shivered in agreement. "No one else has ever made me feel like this."

"It could always be like this."

Cris buried his cock to the hilt, so deep I could hardly think straight as I clawed for purchase upon the desktop. *Always.* I'd never wanted always. I definitely wasn't ready for it with Cris...but I wasn't completely terrified of the idea. Progress.

"More," I whispered. "Touch me. Kiss me. Bite me. I need you everywhere. I need you here, eyes wide open."

"Yes, my sweet."

~

"Bless me, Father, for I have sinned."

My whispered words were lost in the noise of the raging storm outside. The chapel's aged wood creaked and groaned with every gust of wind, as though adding its own pleas to the Almighty. I wasn't convinced that I was safe from the bad weather here, but the small chapel seemed my best bet in sheltering from a demon attack. Even Cris, the lord of the manor, couldn't set foot on the chapel's holy ground. It reminded me of the many abandoned sites I'd scouted for the team—shabby to the point of being hazardous to your health.

I'd never felt so achingly alone in my whole life, and that that worried me—I worshipped my independence, but my anxious stomach twisted into increasing knots as I watched Cris on my tablet, the lone defender patrolling the manor. We'd disabled the transmission so the team couldn't watch. I was an audience of one, waiting for monsters to leap out and attack my boyfriend.

Wait, boyfriend?

I shook the thought away as I huddled in front of the altar, surrounded by lanterns and candles. The tiny building had no electricity, not that it mattered. A terrific crash of thunder had heralded the end of power in the main house an hour ago, leaving the generator to power the gadgets. I tracked the shuffle of Cris's footsteps over my headphones and caught glimpses of his passage on my screen. He murmured words of encouragement over the headset, interspersed with listing things he'd rather be doing with me. I was rather impressed that even though he was in incubus mode he managed to keep it together and focus on protection instead of porn, but I had no doubt that I was going to be pounced and ravished once the coast was clear.

I had set up rem-pods at the manor's entrances for early demon detection, and I flinched at a chorus of high-pitched electronic ringing.

"They're at the mudroom," I warned.

"On my way," he replied.

The camera caught hints of snarling, roiling darkness as Cris engaged the invaders. My hands clenched into fists and my jaw clenched. *Shit.* I wanted to help, but I'd promised to stay in the chapel unless absolutely necessary.

"Should I help?" I asked.

"No. Stay put." He bit the words out between heaving breaths as he fought.

I frowned—Cris had inhuman stamina, but he was a lover, not a fighter. I probably had more self-defense training than he did. Then the blood froze in my veins as Cris loosed an agonized scream.

"Cris? Cris!"

No response, only terrible silence. My heart leaped into my throat as I shoved to my feet, raced to the chapel doors and threw them open. I stared into the black, howling storm, my hands shaking and my mouth dry.

"Come out, little girl. I want to meet Cristóbal's new darling." The woman's voice purred over my headset. Isabel, I presumed.

I took a hesitant step forward, and then shook my head. Oh hell no, I wasn't falling for that shit. I needed a plan, and a weapon. Isabel was expecting a delicate flower, but my father is a Chicago cop and he did not raise shrinking violets. I booked it back to where I'd dropped the tablet and peered at the screen. A wispy shadow paced the kitchen, darkness flowing around her like the skirts of a ball gown.

She paused, and I was nearly deafened by Cris howling in agony. My heart pounded—oh God, she was torturing him. I glanced around in panic, looking for anything I could use for a weapon. I grabbed the cross in front of the altar. It was practically a javelin—a long golden cross atop a metal pole, usually carried into the church by an altar boy as part of the priest's procession. I hefted the weight of the cross in my hands, tucked it under my armpit like a knight about to joust and picked up the sturdiest lantern.

I set one foot across the threshold of the chapel and was immediately blasted by wind and rain. I put my head down and made a beeline for the manor's main entrance. Cris could scold me later for getting mud on the foyer floor, if we both lived. When I arrived in the kitchen several short, stumpy shadow demons milled about. Pygmy demons restrained a struggling Cris, and the air was heavy with the scent of blood. A woman made of darkness smiled at me, her eyes glowing red in the dark. She moved with fluid grace, like a hunting cat, and I hefted the cross and pointed it in her direction.

"Let him go," I ordered.

Isabel laughed. "Why? I am so close to finally owning him completely."

I frowned, unprepared for that response. "What? Why?"

"Cristóbal's tie to this place will end when his last family member passes away. Poor Diego has such little time left, and once he dies, Cristóbal's soul will belong to me."

"Never," Cris growled.

"Silence! I did not give you permission to speak, dog." Isabel had dominatrix potential, but I didn't feel like giving her career advice.

"You knew about this?" I asked. He didn't answer, but Isabel grinned. My stomach twisted into an anxious knot.

"Has my pet been telling lies again?" She tsked and shook her head. "It appears he has learned nothing from his punishment." She backhanded him, and I dropped the lantern and wielded my borrowed cross like a spear.

"Touch him again and I drop you like an 8 a.m. lecture," I warned.

"Such bravery. It's such a pity that—"

"Hey! Stop monologuing, let Cris go, and get the fuck out of here. Now."

Isabel shifted, her red glare fixed on me. "No. He is *mine*. I own his body. Only the blood link has preserved his soul." Isabel grinned, the expression unpleasant. She grabbed a fistful of his hair and yanked his head back, forcing him to look up at her. "I have an eternity of torments prepared for you, my pet."

"He's not your goddamn pet." I pointed the cross in her direction. "Take your freaky pets, go back to whatever shithole you crawled out of, and don't come back."

"You dare—" Isabel stepped toward me and I charged.

"GO TO HELL, YOU FUCKING BITCH!"

The cross crashed into her shoulder and the impact nearly tore it from my grip. Isabel crumpled like the Wicked Witch of the West melting in a shrieking puddle of black skirts, and then poof! She was gone, and her minions too.

Cris collapsed and I rushed to his side, setting the cross close enough to reach but far enough not to accidentally wallop him. "Are you all right?"

He groaned and rolled to his back. I touched his chest and my hands came away stained black with blood. My inner big sister/triage nurse kicked in. "Where is your first aid kit?"

"Blue powder room."

Good, that was close. "Stay here."

I grabbed the lantern and dashed off. I scrubbed my hands clean like a doctor prepping for surgery. Armed with the kit, I returned to Cris's side.

"You banished her," Cris said. "I doubt she was expecting that."

"Well, she better get used to disappointment." I touched the wound and he hissed. "How bad is it?"

"I will survive," he assured me.

"Damn right you will, because you have some serious explaining to do." Several deep gouges were torn across his torso.

Luckily I had super glue in my bag—faster and neater than stitches. "How long before she comes back?"

"She won't be back tonight. It may take her a few days to regain her strength, because she was unprepared."

"Good. That'll give us time to plan. Hold still. This is going to hurt."

He caught my hand and held it tight. "Nati..."

"Damn it, Cris. What part of 'the whole truth and nothing but the truth' did you not understand? It's pretty fucking simple."

"I did not wish to worry you."

"Bullshit." I splashed antiseptic over his wounds and he howled in pain. I felt slightly guilty—but only slightly.

"I have not told anyone, not even Diego. There was nothing he could do."

"Do you really think I can save you, or were you feeding me lines to keep me here so you could have one last hurrah?"

"I would never—"

"*¡Cállate!*" I snapped. "Hush while I play doctor."

I cleaned, glued and dressed his wounds, then helped him into a sitting position, only to discover more wounds on his back. I swallowed hard as my temper cracked and fear crept in. "Is there some kind of demon emergency room we can call for you?" I asked, anxiety threaded through my voice.

"No. It will be all right. Magicians heal quickly."

"You're not quite a magician now though, right? Because of the curse?"

Cris wheezed and shuddered. I abandoned arguing in favor of another round of first aid. By the time I finished he looked like a reverse Dalmatian, and I eased him to his feet. We started the slow, stumbling journey to his bedroom in the cellar, and I was exhausted by the time I tucked him into bed.

He caught my hand. "Stay with me."

"No." My hand was pale against the busy darkness clouding his skin—which was something, because I'd never been pale, not even in January in Chicago. I tugged it free and stepped out of reach.

"Please, Nati."

"Nope. Not nearly enough groveling." I dragged a chair from its spot in front of the fireplace, placed it next to the bed and plopped into it.

"You fought for me."

"I fought for us," I blurted before the realizing the weight of those words. I winced as I scrambled to change the subject. "If you're right that she won't be back for a couple of days, we need to buckle down on curing you. So how do we end this curse? It's sort of *Beauty and the Beast*. Is there an enchanted rose somewhere around here?"

"No? Are you calling me a beast?"

"Well you're ravenous, you growl and you make poor life choices." I peered at him. "It's a fairy tale. Disney redid it a few years ago. You've never seen it? It was one of their biggest hits."

"I don't often watch animated movies."

"They did a live action remake. We're watching it when we have time. You'll like it. Big, mysterious mansion. Giant library. In the Disney movie the Beast was cursed into a big, furry, werewolf-like form by a witch. Apparently he was rude to her, because he was all rich and spoiled and had white privilege." Cris quirked a brow, but I continued. "In order to break the curse he needed to learn how to love, and to be loved."

Cris snorted. "Loving is what got me into this mess."

"No, fucking is what got you into this mess." I wagged a scolding finger. "The hot, crazy chick may be fun to fool around with, but it always ends bad. You can't fix crazy."

"This is true. I did learn the lesson in enough time to realize that I should marry another, but by then it was too late."

"Did you love Angela?"

"I admired her. Love was not often a factor in marriage of wealthy families. It was a business arrangement."

"It still is, in some places. My parents are crazy in love with each other. It helped them get through some tough times. They were an odd match for their generation, and that made us odd kids. We never fit in anywhere."

"You would fit in here."

"In the haunted house? Doubtful."

"With me. I won't stay here if I am freed. This house...there are too many memories here. It is a lovely prison, but it is a prison all the same."

"You really can't leave?" I asked. "You've never hopped in a car and told someone to drive?"

"A car? No. I tried many times to walk off the property, and each time I was overwhelmed by pain and sickness. Once I collapsed, and awoke in my bed with no idea of how I'd gotten there. After time, I gave up." He sighed. "It is a curse to be forever young, and to watch generations of your family wither and die."

"I'm sorry." I meant it. I hated the idea of Cris's suffering. I wanted to be able to hold him and make everything better, but somehow I doubted that the curse could be solved so easily. In *Beauty and the Beast* it took a great act of love and sacrifice. I had the hots for Cris, and I cared about him, but I didn't love him. Lust was easy, but love took time and effort. We weren't going to get anywhere while we had trust issues.

## CHAPTER THIRTEEN

The doorbell rang—at least I assumed it was the doorbell, because I'd never heard the thing before. I yelped and dropped the voice recorder, and it bounced beneath the bed.

"Oops. Umm, Nati dropped the recorder after the bell rang," I said to mark the spot. Then I crouched down, picked it up and turned it off. "I guess I should answer it, huh?"

"What'd you do, order a pizza?" Kenji asked.

"At one a.m.? No," I replied. "I don't think they have pizza in Spain."

"Take the handcam with you, in case it's paranormal," he added. "And the lantern, in case it's a shadow demon."

"Shadow demons who ring doorbells? Really? Pretty sure they're not that polite." I shook my head in disbelief. In fact after my throwdown with Isabel last night I knew they weren't that polite.

Cris and I had spent the day in his library, pulling books on banishing spells and diving into our research. I didn't understand all of the magical details, but the research methodology was the same. I took copious notes, which Cris was currently reviewing while I stumbled around in the dark looking for signs of my Tía

Angela. She had been silent so far—probably hiding in case Isabel invaded again. I didn't blame her.

"Land shark?" he guessed.

"Kenji, if you try telling me that land sharks are real, I will slap you through the internet." I walked to the main entrance and opened the door to find two people standing on the front step. Judging by their clothing I half expected them to say trick-or-treat, or ask for directions to a rave.

"Turn the cameras off," the woman said, in English.

I blinked. "What?"

"We don't come in until the cameras are off," she said. "Who's on your headset? John?"

"No, Kenji."

"Who are you talking to?" Kenji asked.

"No idea, but she seems to know you."

"Me? What did I do?"

"Tell him have no fear, Patience is here," she said dryly. "Then hang up. Cameras off, headset off. All the gadgets go off before we come in." She folded her arms and waited.

Okay then. I repeated her words to Kenji, who groaned in disappointment. "Aww, man. If she exorcises the place we'll have nothing left to investigate."

"I'm so glad you're concerned with my safety. How do you know her?"

"She's the best demonologist we've ever worked with," he said.

Ah. This was Piper's contact. About time.

"Got it. Good night, Kenji." I turned off the headset and then nodded to my guests. "I'm Nati, by the way. And you're Patience?"

"Yes. I'm Patience Roberts, and this is my husband, Faust."

"Nice to meet you. Okay, gadgets off. I'll be right back."

It took ten minutes to shut down all the cameras, recorders and detectors, but I felt better with most of the lights on again. I returned to the front door to find my guests mid-cuddle. Geez. Piper did mention that they were on their honeymoon. Patience was a tall woman with bright, cherry red hair and stunning green eyes. Her husband was slightly shorter than her, with spiky black hair and the palest blue eyes I'd ever seen. He was dressed in a conservative black business suit, but Patience was wearing red and black leather, including a long black coat like she had arrived via the Matrix.

I cleared my throat politely, and they parted.

"Everything off?" Patience asked.

"Yes, but I'm not sure I'm allowed to let you in. The contract allowing me to investigate here is only if I'm alone."

Faust waved a dismissive hand. "We are not human, and thus technically not legal people."

"I..." I stared at them, stunned silent. Not human? What the hell were they? Holograms?

"Aha. I see your demon problem." Patience peered over my shoulder into the hallway behind me, and I turned and spotted Cris in the shadows, watching. "Well, fuck a duck, the team bagged a big one this time."

"No, not that one. He's not the problem," I replied. "He's on my side, but he's supposed to be in the library doing his homework like we agreed."

"He must've done a number on you. Let Auntie Patience fix it." Patience stepped forward and I splayed my arms wide, blocking her access to the hallway.

"Whoa! Don't touch him," I snapped. "Or me either. If you can't handle that, you can just turn around and go back to honeymooning."

"That's unusual." Faust pensively stroked an imaginary beard as he studied me. "Don't they usually want to get rid of the demon, not keep it?"

"Depends on the demon," Patience replied. "It doesn't take much for an incubus to ensnare a mortal."

"Hey, I'm not ensnared, and he's only sort of an incubus," I countered.

"I have used no magic on Natividad," Cris said. Both of our guests seemed startled by his voice, or maybe by his accented

English. "I would never harm her. And she is correct that I am not a natural incubus. I assume that you are a summoner?"

Patience shrugged. "Got it in one, but I'm retired. I'm a faerie now. Faeries are cool." She turned to Faust. "Now *that* is unusual. Most incubi are all, 'Hey baby, wanna wrestle?' Not so much with the polite conversation."

I blinked, wondering if I'd heard that wrong. She was a faerie? She looked so...well, not necessarily normal per se, but human. Huh. Weren't faeries supposed to be Tinker Bell–sized, with wings and pixie dust?

"Okay then." Patience balled her hands on her hips. "I'm going to put a human glamour over you for a bit so you can come out and talk like a civilized person. And some clothes, too, because if you point your incubus stick at me my sweetie's going to flip his lid." She cracked her knuckles, and then with a snap of her fingers Cris looked like himself again, tight jeans and all.

Cris stepped forward to embrace me but then he paused, likely remembering that he was still in the doghouse. "Are you all right?"

"Fine. I think I broke their voice recorder when I dropped it though."

"I will replace it," he promised.

Patience flopped onto the loveseat and patted the cushion beside her for her husband. Faust sat at his wife's side and slid a possessive arm around her shoulders. With another snap of her fingers a fresh pot of coffee appeared on the table between us, complete with cream, sugar and four bright red mugs. "I'm a little confused. You two seem to be getting along, and the team made it sound like there was imminent, life-threatening peril about to happen here."

"There is. Just not from him." I patted Cris's hand as we sat across from the couple. "Tell them your story."

I helped myself to a cup of black coffee—I needed all the angry caffeine I could get—as Cris began his tale. Patience and Faust listened with rapt interest as he explained how Isabel had murdered Angela and cursed him into his demonic state. When Cris finished, Patience turned to Faust.

"I wonder if Simon knows anything about this. He would've been in England still when the curse went down, yeah?" Patience said.

"France then, I believe."

"Even better. Librarians are a pretty close-knit community. Gossip like this had to have spread."

"Yes," Faust agreed. "At the very least he should have a record of it."

"Simon?" I asked.

"My stepson. He's a chronicler," Patience explained. I turned to Cris to clarify.

"A chronicler is an immortal librarian who serves the Order of St. Jerome. I was pursuing being apprenticed to a chronicler when I was cursed."

Right, hence the St. Jerome medal that I was still carrying around in my pocket. I should probably return it, but I frowned at the idea.

Faust kissed Patience. "I will speak with him. Stay out of trouble while I'm gone."

"You'll be gone for five minutes. How much trouble can I get into? Wait, don't answer that," she ordered Faust. He chuckled and vanished into thin air.

"Holy shit." My jaw dropped. "What just happened?"

"He's a faerie too," Patience explained. "We teleport. Though Faust and I are a little different from your average faeries. You know you can't tell the *Spirit Seekers* crew any of this, right? I mean, they can chase all the light anomalies and disembodied whispers that they want, but the big stuff is out of their league. That's where I come in. The nonmagical majority is happier living in blissful ignorance of the real things that go bump in the night who can seriously kick their asses."

"Yes, we've already established that," Cris said.

"I still don't like it, but I understand the need for it," I said. "As much as I'd like to think we've evolved as a species, I've read the comments sections on the internet, and no, we really haven't. The team is excited about the things they've found on this investigation, but it's still blurry shadows and weird noises. Nothing big."

"Good." She tilted her head and studied me over the rim of her red mug. A black diamond decorated it, like a playing card or Harley Quinn.

"May I ask, how did you become a faerie?" Cris asked. "I have never heard of such a thing."

"Neither did I, until it happened. Turns out that Faust is my soul mate, and he's a faerie. I died, more or less, and instead of becoming a demon—that's a summoner thing, as you've heard," she said to me, "I became a faerie."

"Soul mates are a real thing too?" I asked.

"Yes, but they're extremely rare." She chugged her coffee and then refilled her mug with a wave of her hand. "But it's a very good thing that I'm still alive and kicking, because there's been major demon activity lately. We're still learning all the details about it. And there was a mass-murder-slash-abduction of American summoners. No summoners to police the demon population means more demon incursions. I'm the last summoner standing in the Midwest, so shit got real in Chicago over the past few months. We're on the verge of a demon apocalypse."

I straightened as fear iced my veins. "My parents live in Chicago. Most of my family is there. Are they in danger? Should I warn them somehow?"

"We can add them to the watch list. Keep an eye out for them."

"Thank you."

"De nada." She turned to Cris and studied him. "I figure that Isabel wants to add you to her list of minions, because having a former librarian would give her an edge in whatever the demons are up to. She's probably super pissed that Nati is interfering with her plans."

"Great." I sighed. "How do we stop her?"

"If you want to kill her you'll have to find out where she lives and go to the source, and, no offense, you don't strike me as the demon-slaying sort."

"I will vanquish Isabel," Cris said.

She snorted. "No you won't. Not while she's holding your ticket. One word from her and you'll do whatever she orders. You could try hiring a summoner to kill her for you, but it'll be a bitch and a half to find one crazy enough to do it, who is also powerful enough and within your price range. And no, we're not talking dollars or euros. You'd just find yourself in debt to him instead of Isabel. And before you ask, I can't do it either. Faeries and the shadow realm don't mix for more than a few minutes, and that's not long enough to kill her."

"I understand. But Isabel isn't a true demon," Cris argued. "She was human once. Her home realm is here. Will that enable us to defeat her?"

"Hmm. Actually I've never encountered that before. Good question. Once a summoner flips, we don't hear from them again. The general thought is that the summoner either doesn't remember her previous life, or other demons make her their bitch as payback for whatever she did during her summoner days." Patience shuddered. "So glad I avoided that fate. Remind me to kiss Faust when he gets back."

"Like you need a reminder." I changed the subject. "You don't really think that there'll be a demon apocalypse, do you?"

"Not on my watch." Patience grinned. "But if there is, it'll really chap the asses of everyone who was preparing for zombies."

I shook my head, then rubbed the skin between my eyes. All this was giving me an epic headache. Maybe this was some elaborate network stunt. A special episode of *Spirit Seekers*, where they trolled the skeptic until she believed in God, magic and demon apocalypses. Apocalypsi? Ugh.

"How did you end up working with *Spirit Seekers*?" I asked, changing the subject again.

"Divine providence, I suppose. Investigators do run into real demons on occasion. A priest introduced the Chicagoland team to me, and after that I had every chapter in their international Scooby squad calling me with questions. It's worked out all right. It saves the teams from getting really hurt. When demons start pushing them around, they know to call me to take care of it."

"Seems like they'd be excited to catch that kind of activity during an investigation."

"Yes and no. They don't want to endanger their crew, or the people who live in the houses they investigate. A few claw marks and growls make for good television, but stirring up a demon without deporting it can have serious consequences. Like in Amityville, when that possessed bastard killed his wife and kids with a rifle. Bestselling books and major motion pictures are bad news for the magical community. And those Warren quacks inspired a whole generation of paranormal investigators. The straights outnumber magicians. They nearly wiped us out once thanks to witch hunts. They could do it again."

I fidgeted and frowned. My life revolved around my need to unearth hidden history, and to bring light to stories that had been covered up or forgotten. I might spontaneously combust from the frustration of not being able to tell the world about what I'd found, but I also understood that the world wasn't as tolerant as it should be. Even in the twenty-first century people were murdered every day for being the "wrong" color, religion, or sexual identity.

"There might come a time when we can't hide anymore." Patience set her mug down. "I hope it's not soon."

"Can you... I apologize if this is rude or too forward, but I'm dying to know just what a faerie is. Can you do something faerie-ish so I can see?" I asked.

"Like what? Burst into song with a flock of talking mice?"

"Yes."

Patience laughed. "Here, I'll show you my new favorite thing."

She rose and walked a few steps away from the loveseat. She glanced behind her as though checking to see if the coast was clear, and suddenly an enormous pair of flaming butterfly wings sprouted from her back like a firework. She flexed the wings for dramatic effect as my jaw dropped.

"Fiera?" Cris said. It wasn't a word I recognized, but Patience nodded.

"You're good at this. Then again that's a librarian's job, I suppose."

"That's amazing," I said.

"I know, right?" Patience doused her wings and returned to her seat, and then we chatted a bit about less dramatic things until Faust returned.

The faerie popped into the room, and our coffee set vanished and was replaced with a pile of books so high and heavy that the table groaned beneath its weight. Cris and I rose in order to see Patience over the top of the stack.

"Simon had not heard of this tale," Faust said, "but he had an earful of complaints about how the Order was run in Spain. It sounds as though they may have covered up this situation. Unfortunately, he does not currently have time to aid in your research, but he is lending you these books from his collection to supplement your own research."

Cris sighed in relief. "Thank you, Don Faust. I am grateful to him, and you and Doña Patience."

"He also suggests that Patience fortify the wards around your manor to keep further demon incursions at bay," Faust said.

"I can do that, no problem," Patience said.

Eyes wide, I stared at the mountain of magical literature. "This would take weeks to go through."

"You don't have weeks," Patience said. "Read fast. I like working with the *Seekers*. I want to keep their people alive and happy, so try not to die."

Our guests vanished and I stared at the books, my shaking hands folded behind my back. *Try not to die.* Easier said than done. If I'd known about Isabel, would I have been so quick to agree to help Cris? If he couldn't fight her, it was really all on me. Was I strong enough to do this?

"Natividad," he murmured.

"This is a lot to process. I don't know what to do."

"You don't need to do anything. You can contact your team and return to your investigation if you wish. I will leave you in peace."

I winced, my eyes squeezed shut. "Oh shit. I forgot about the team. We were trying to make progress with Angela. I should go to the command center. After we bring these downstairs."

Cris placed a tentative hand on my shoulder. "It's going to be all right, Nati."

"I want to believe that. I really do. But it's all gone topsy-turvy. I flew into this country a skeptic and an atheist. I was completely happy with my life the way it was. Now..."

"I won't allow any harm to come to you," he assured me.

"You can't promise that." I moved away from his touch and rubbed my arms as though I felt a draft. "One word from Isabel and you'll turn on me."

"There are steps we can take to counteract that. We don't need to act right this moment. We can speak about it in the morning after you have rested and I am myself again."

"Oh. Right. I forgot that you're all shadowy now. That spell of hers worked really well." I cleared my throat. "Let's clean this up, and then I'm going to investigate."

"Of course." Cris took a purposeful step away, out of arm's reach. "Nati...I do not deserve your help. I know that. I gave you my word, and then I broke it. I have committed many terrible sins since my curse, and—"

"And some of that you're not responsible for," I interrupted. "Isabel is. Your curse led you to do the things you did. Like being a puppet, having your strings pulled by someone else."

"That doesn't absolve me of those sins."

The corners of my mouth twitched. "The church would. Absolve you, that is. In Catholicism all you have to do is repent and all is forgiven. Maybe say the rosary a few times."

"I doubt that they would forgive being a demon."

"Well, it's a good thing I'm not a Catholic anymore then. I forgive you."

Cris's eyes widened as though stunned. "I...thank you."

"But"—I paused and pointed at him for dramatic effect—"*you* made the decision to get involved with her, and then *you* made the decision to break up with her. I'm sure you handled it badly considering that it pushed all her psycho buttons. I don't believe that you deserved to be cursed, but you need to own your responsibility for your actions."

"I know."

"No, you don't know, because you're still making the same mistakes."

He scowled. "And you aren't, Señora Americana?"

"What the hell is that supposed to mean?" I stepped closer and he stepped back.

"What are you running from?" he asked.

"I'm not—"

"No?" This time he moved in and I moved away, like we were doing some sort of argument tango. "You ran from your faith, your family. You keep everyone at arm's length. Why? So nothing will ever hurt you again? You're so opposed to putting down roots that you're like the wind, never resting."

I scrubbed my face with my hands. "Jesus, you sound like my mother. I'd rather be the wind than stuck in one place like a potted plant. Okay. Seriously leaving this time. You can move the books your own damn self." I hightailed it from the room before we could delve further into the realm of blame and forgiveness.

# CHAPTER FOURTEEN

I sat at the dressing mirror and stared at my bedraggled reflection. All these late hours had given me awful dark circles under my eyes. My reflection hardly looked like me—I looked lost. Haunted. The irony of the word sent me into a fit of hysterical giggles.

Magic. Demons, curses, ghosts. When had my life veered so far off the beaten path that I barely recognized myself anymore?

Oh yeah, when I came to Spain. Or rather, when I'd started digging up my family's history. Maybe I should have let sleeping dogs lie, but if I had, Cris would've been doomed to serve the Bitch Queen once Diego passed away. My research led me here, like I was fulfilling my destiny. Too bad said destiny didn't come with instructions—to defeat the wicked witch, just add water! After two days of researching our borrowed books we pieced together roughly eighty percent of the spell we needed to sever the link between Cris and Isabel. After that, the plan was to slay her or banish her, whichever worked. We needed more time, but our time was just about up.

I sighed and turned to the silent room.

"Hi, again," I addressed Angela's spirit. "It's still me, Natividad.

I'm not recording anything now, in case you were worried about that."

No response. Not that I'd been expecting one—she had been quiet since she led me to the ledger. I continued.

"I'm sorry about what happened to you. I know that doesn't help you. Well, maybe it helps to know you're not forgotten. Cris never forgot you. He helped me tend to your grave. It looks nice now, but those roses were out to get me." I raised my hands to display the war wounds I'd received fighting the rosebushes. "Now I'm helping him break his curse. You probably noticed that. It's going to be one last battle with Isabel, and..."

I fidgeted with my hairbrush, pushing it around on the dressing table until it lined up perfectly with my travel cosmetics case. "It doesn't look good. I might end up as your new ghostly roommate." I smiled dryly. "And here I've spent so much time focused on living alone. Cris was right about one thing. I do push everyone away. I'm terrified of being tied down. My mother is a saint. She's given all her time and energy to her family, and never does anything for herself. I spent my childhood trying to make her life easier by taking care of my younger siblings, and I saw myself becoming her. I didn't want to end up married and living in a three-bedroom house with nine people and a dog in it. I wanted...more. I wanted to see the world."

I sighed and rubbed my eyes wearily. "I guess I was selfish. Maybe Cris and I are alike that way. He thought he could play with fire with his crazy mistress, but he got burned. I got burned and I've been running away from that pain ever since. I need to stop trying to convince myself that I'm happy with what I have and figure out what actually makes me happy. And hell, maybe Cris and I can figure things out together. It'd be nice to have the chance..."

I trailed off, and the room stayed silent. "I don't know. I want us all to find peace and a happy ending. I guess we'll see how that works out." My laugh was thin and brittle like early winter ice. "Like a fairy tale. I never thought of myself as the fairy-tale type. I didn't want magic in my life, yet here it is. Anyway, that's all I have to say."

I climbed into bed and tugged a pillow over my eyes, and as I dropped off into an exhausted sleep I thought I heard a soft sigh.

When I entered the kitchen the following morning I discovered a note from Cris informing me that breakfast would be served in the gazebo. I waved at the camera in the kitchen and then headed outside. A tray of fruit and pastries awaited me along with a carafe of coffee, and I smiled. I enjoyed a quiet meal, listening to the unfamiliar song of Spanish birds. The view would have been more pleasant if the blooms in the garden hadn't been shredded by the wind and rain from the storm a few nights ago. The roses that had lasted this long were now barren, and the carpet of muddy petals added a melancholy air to my meal.

Cris arrived as I was sipping my second cup of coffee, and he handed me a single rosebud. "It was the only one to survive the storm. I wanted you to have it, because it won't survive the first frost."

"Thank you." I took the flower and blushed. Pretty sure the last time I got flowers from a man was at senior prom, when Brian got me a wrist corsage.

"How are you feeling today?" Cris asked.

"I'm okay. I didn't sleep very well."

"I would've been happy to help with that." He grinned, and I chuckled.

"I bet." I sipped my coffee and studied him. We'd settled into a sort of wary truce while we researched the spell. He hadn't tried to seduce me, and while I appreciated the respect for my space I did miss the amazing sex.

"If I can do magic, will you teach me?" I asked.

"Of course. Though it is unlikely that you are a librarian, as I was. There are several types of magician. You could be a witch, or..." He trailed off, his brow furrowed.

"What?"

"A summoner. You might be a summoner. That would enable you to defeat Isabel."

I blinked. "I thought you said summoners were evil?"

"The greedy ones are, and sadly they are all too common." Cris sighed and ran a hand through his hair. "But there are summoners who concentrate on banishing demons. It sounds as though that is the sort of work Patience has been doing for your *Spirit Seeker* friends."

I wrinkled my nose. "Hopefully this will be my one and only demon-slaying adventure. I'd much rather be a librarian."

"You would be excellent at it. I have been impressed with your research skills."

"Speaking of which, we should get back to the grind. We're burning daylight." I chugged the rest of my coffee and rose.

"Of course. Nati..." He paused and looked away. "Whatever happens tonight, I want you to know how grateful I am for our time together, and how sorry I am that I hurt you."

"Thank you." I offered a hand and helped him rise, and then I kissed him on the cheek. Emotion swelled in my chest and tightened my throat as I met his gaze. I had a million things to say, and no idea how to say them. Romantic words hadn't been part of my vocabulary for a very long time. I settled for wrapping my arms around him and holding him tight. "It's going to be okay."

"I hope so." He brushed a kiss against my hair, and then he drew away, smiling and shaking his head.

"What's so funny?"

"Hope," he said. "I had given up on hope long ago. I thought Diego's plan might bring peace to Angela, but never to me."

I rolled my shoulders and stood tall. "Well, we're going to do our best."

# CHAPTER FIFTEEN

We chose the ballroom as the venue for our showdown—it was large enough to fight in and it housed the least amount of breakable things. I was amused by Cris's concern for the safety of the furniture, but I'd probably form attachments to it if I was trapped in the same place for a few centuries. All of the *Spirit Seekers* equipment had been taken down and returned to its storage containers, because no matter what the outcome of this battle was, the investigation would definitely be over. We had more than enough footage for an episode, so the network would be pleased. It wasn't easy to explain to the team why I'd called an early end to my adventures and still preserve the sanctity of magician society, so I laid the blame at Patience Roberts's feet and claimed that she was exorcising the place because things had become too dangerous. I doubted that she would mind.

"Are you ready?" Cris asked. He was in his incubus form, and his words sent heat spiraling through my core. Great. That was a distraction I did not need. I was already avoiding looking at him in all his shadowy, naked glory.

"As I'll ever be," I said.

"Good. I will cast the protective circle."

Said protective circle was a magical barrier that would keep us safe from attack and protect Cris from Isabel's influence. He was pouring all his magical strength into the circle, so once it was finished he was out of the fight except for providing moral support.

Cris picked up a ritual dagger and pointed it at the floor, using it as a guide to mark the boundary of the circle. I watched his feet as he walked the edge. I was a little disappointed that I couldn't see anything magical—I was hoping for shiny special effects, but no such luck. When he made a complete circuit I felt a snap of static electricity as the spell set.

Now all we had to do was wait.

Cris sat beside me, took my hand and squeezed it. "You'll be fine."

I nodded but didn't trust my voice enough to answer as anxiety tingled up and down my arms and tightened my chest. I could do this. The completed ritual reminded me a bit too much of the church—candles, incense, chanting, same old same old. Even the Latin was easier to read aloud than I thought it would be, thanks to my Catholic upbringing and my fluency in Spanish.

Several loud crashes sounded from the first floor below us and Cris flinched.

"Duct tape," I blurted.

"I'm sorry?"

"Duct tape fixes everything. It's like the Force. It has a light side and a dark side, and it binds the universe together."

Cris barked a quick laugh, but then the ballroom doors burst open and the candles outside of the circle whooshed out. Isabel sailed into the room, and directly into our trap.

A ward snapped into place the moment she crossed the threshold, keeping her in and her servants out. She shrieked in outrage, and I snickered.

"You will pay for that," Isabel snapped.

"Bite me," I said. I picked up my script and started to chant. Everything sounded more dramatic in Latin, and it helped me get into character. I might not end up Natividad Houlihan, PhD, but Mistress of Magic had a nice ring to it.

Isabel hissed like a pissed-off feral cat and rushed the circle. She shrieked again as she bounced off the barrier—really she had a future as a banshee if this demon thing didn't work out—and she pounded it with her fists.

"Your magic is weak, Cristóbal. This will not hold me."

Cris rose and stared Isabel down. "It only has to hold long enough."

She struck the barrier again and this time I flinched as bright sparks erupted from the spot where she'd hit it. I kept chanting, because I had several verses, a bridge and a recurring chorus left to go before the spell was complete.

Isabel paced, testing the circle for weak spots. "Why do you fight me, my pet? You wanted me more than anything once. Is it truly so terrible to do so again?"

"I was a fool," Cris said, "and you are a monster. I will never serve you."

"You will grovel at my feet like a dog and thank me for the honor." Another hit, and the barrier began to glow with a soft white light where she attacked it. That couldn't be a good sign.

"Never!"

Isabel struck the circle again and black cracks spread through the energy like poison. The glow thinned where the shadows concentrated.

I stumbled in the chant but recovered quickly and read faster.

"Isabel, stop it," Cris snapped, and she smiled.

"No! You deserve to be punished. The first thing I will order you to do is execute your lover." She struck again and the energy fractured with an audible crack like breaking glass.

"No!" Cris howled, his voice filled with agony. My gut twisted at the realization that the barrier would fall before I could finish the spell. Cris turned and I risked a glance at him. He smiled weakly.

"Forgive me, *mi corazón*." He picked up the ritual dagger and stabbed it into his heart.

The air was filled with screams—mine, his and Isabel's. Cris crumpled, and the shadows fled his skin as his life bled away. I abandoned the spell and dove for him, which saved me from being walloped in the head by Isabel as she surged past the circle's edge. I rolled away and stumbled to my feet.

"You wretch," Isabel spat. "I waited centuries for my revenge and you spoiled it."

"Deal with it, bitch." I balanced on the balls of my feet, waiting for her to pounce. I didn't have a single weapon on me, just the St. Jerome medal in my pocket.

Metal clattered beside me, and I spotted a shovel toppling to the ballroom floor. What the actual fuck? I didn't have time to wonder where it came from, and I grabbed the wooden handle with both hands and wielded it before me like a bo staff. Isabel rushed with blind fury and I smacked her square in the face—if she'd been human she would've been missing some teeth.

Stunned, she reeled away, and I shifted my grip and swung the shovel like a baseball bat. Isabel went sprawling, but then she threw a hand out and hit me with a magical whammy that sent me sailing through the air. I had an inane moment to wonder if this was how it felt when faeries flew, and then I crashed into the wall behind me and saw stars as my head cracked against the lovely paneling. I landed with a thud that knocked the air from my lungs.

Isabel giggled. "Pathetic human. Did you really think you could defeat me?"

Shit. She was going to monologue me to death. I flipped her off and she scowled.

"Enough of this."

I tensed as Isabel moved in for the kill, but then an oil painting depicting a lovely landscape leaped off the wall and clobbered her. She shrieked, tangled in canvas and a gilded frame, and I used her distraction as my opening. I lurched to my feet, yanked the silver St. Jerome medal from my pocket with one hand and grabbed her arm with the other. A bright white light beamed from the medal, and I squinted as it blinded me.

"Go to hell, and don't come back," I shouted.

The demon howled in agony and my skin burned where I gripped her, but I held on tight as she tried to squirm out of my grasp. For a moment I thought the banishment hadn't worked, but then my fingers closed as Isabel vanished and the light faded. The ruined painting clattered to the floor, and I blinked rapidly to restore my vision.

A gauzy white figure hovered in my periphery, one slender arm pointed toward the spot where Cris had fallen. I turned and the image was gone, but I followed her lead. I ran to Cris and kneeled at his side.

I cursed, my shaking hands hovering over his body as I panicked over what to do. Should I pull the knife? He'd definitely bleed out if I did, but I doubted that he could heal with a blade in his heart. I said a quick prayer, yanked the knife free and pressed my hands against the wound to stanch the bleeding. When that clearly wasn't going to work I tugged my shirt off and used it as a bandage.

"Don't you dare die on me, Cris," I warned. My voice was choked with tears and I blinked burning eyes. "You stupid idiot. Why did you have to go selfless on me now? I almost had her."

But I hadn't, and he knew that. He sacrificed himself to save me.

"Don't go. Please don't go." But Cris was silent and still, and I knew it was too late. My control broke and I started sobbing—the sort of heartbroken ugly cry that I swore I'd never suffer through again. But this situation called for it, because I was gutted. Hollowed out. I hadn't realized how badly I wanted to spend my life with him until that door had closed.

I slumped over him. It wasn't fair. I failed—I let my damsel down, just when he'd finally learned from his mistakes and I'd learned how to trust again. We deserved the chance to see the world together. I'd finally have someone to share my adventures with, someone who loved history as much as I did. Damn it, we were so close, too. A few more seconds and the spell would've worked. But no, I was the worst hero ever.

"I'm so sorry," I whispered against his chest. I was so mired in my misery that I didn't notice the feel of his arms around me until Cris spoke.

"Don't cry."

My breath caught on a miserable hiccup. I sat up and raised my bloody hands to wipe my eyes but thought better of it before I made my vision worse. I wiped my hands on my jeans before rubbing my eyes.

Cris was alive—awake, alive and watching me with completely human eyes. My jaw dropped.

"Is this real?" I blurted. He smiled and my heart soared. "How?"

"To be honest, I have no idea. I think I heard you calling for me, and I knew I could not leave you. You brought me back."

I pushed my bloody T-shirt aside and gasped—the wound was gone, completely healed shut.

"I...so we won?" I asked.

"Yes." He chuckled and winced. "I am somewhat sore, however."

"Better sore than dead. Does this mean I have magic?"

"I believe so."

Holy cow. Magic and a Spanish god of sex. And it wasn't even my birthday.

"You need pants," I said.

Cris quirked an eyebrow. "Do I?"

I laughed. "Maybe not. We definitely need a shower. It looks like we survived a slasher film."

"Agreed."

I helped him stand, and he immediately drew me into his arms and kissed me. "I love you, Natividad."

"I love you, too." I clung to him, afraid to let go. "You're free. Where should we go first? After we celebrate," I amended.

"Perhaps we could go to Chicago, and you can introduce me to your family."

I blinked away a fresh round of tears—happy ones this time. "I'd like that."

"But before we go, I would like to visit Diego in the hospital," Cris said. "It will do him good to know that his clever plan was successful."

I grinned. "Absolutely"

# EPILOGUE

The used bookstore looked out of place for downtown Naperville, which was filled with trendy boutiques, fine dining and more coffee shops than anyone ever needed.

"This is it?" I asked as I climbed out of the driver's seat of our rental car. I shivered as a blast of wind tried to rip the knit Bears cap off my head. It was early December, but it already felt like mid-January. I really missed the rain in Spain.

Cris shrugged. "It is what the card says."

When Patience and Faust returned to collect our borrowed spellbooks, she handed me a business card. "Next time you're in the Chicagoland area, go here and as for Anne Williams. Tell her we sent you, and that you need your magic identified."

The faeries had also gifted Cris with a new identity and accompanying documentation, which had allowed us to sail through the airport without anyone batting an eyelash. Thus here we were, surrounded by the bustling weekend shopping crowd as they hunted for Christmas bargains. I didn't need a present this year—I already had everything I needed.

I joined Cris on the sidewalk, and we entered the store hand in hand. We both inhaled the heavenly smell of old books and grinned the same goofy smile, and my heart swelled. I loved this man.

An elderly gentleman with glasses and a tweed jacket sat behind the counter.

"He reminds me of Diego," Cris murmured.

"We'll have to tell him when we call later."

Cris nodded. We called Diego once a day to check in. His health was stable, and before we left we arranged for in-home care now that Cris was away. Diego loved hearing all about Cris's adventures.

The gentleman set his paper down, a copy of today's *Daily Herald*. Pfft. Suburban news. Boring. "Can I help you find something?"

"Is Anne Williams here?" I asked.

"What does this pertain to?"

The corners of my mouth twitched. "Patience and Faust sent us."

"Ah." He nodded. "She's in the back office. Just knock on the door."

We walked past aisles of books with labels like "numerology" and "astral projection." I turned to Cris. "Is that for real?"

He smiled. "No. If they have spellbooks here, they are well hidden and available only to a certain clientele."

"Got it."

We arrived at the office door and knocked as instructed. It opened to reveal Anne Williams, who appeared so normal that I never would have pegged her for having some sort of magic ability. She was petite and blonde and about my age, and she wore a tweed pencil skirt, dark tights and a long-sleeved turtleneck sweater. She looked like a grade school teacher, not a magician.

"Can I help you?" she asked. I introduced us both and repeated the message the faeries had given me, and Anne nodded. "Right. I was wondering when you would be by. She wants to hire you."

"What?" I blurted.

"To do what?" Cris asked.

She waved us to step inside the office and closed the door. "I'm getting ahead of myself. May I see your hand please?"

"Umm, sure."

"You're a seer," Cris said, his voice tinged with wonder.

"Yes. She didn't mention that?" Anne said. "No matter." She held her hand out to take mine, and I obliged, curious. She closed her eyes for a few moments, and then she took a deep breath and stepped away. Anne wobbled for a moment and steadied herself on the edge of her desk, and she waved Cris away when he tried to help her.

"Are you well?" he asked.

"I'm good, no worries." She took another deep breath and smiled. "Librarian."

"Really?"

"Really," she confirmed.

Cris whooped, picked me up, spun me and then kissed me.

"Patience still wants to hire you," Anne said when we came up for air. "She needs assistants."

"To do what? She's a faerie," I said.

"Banish demons."

"Oh no," I said. "No way."

"Why does she need librarians to banish demons?" Cris asked.

"She doesn't." Anne shrugged. "But any magician can banish a demon, and you two have experience, plus, and I'm paraphrasing, you owe her one."

I grimaced and turned to Cris. "What do you think?"

He scratched his chin, his brow furrowed. "A demon apocalypse would put a damper on our travel plans."

"Right." I took his hand and squeezed it. We could do this. I felt like I could take on the whole damn world with Cris by my side.

He raised my hand to his lips and kissed it, and then he turned to Anne. "When do we start?"

"Now, probably. Oh, and congratulations."

"On what?" I asked.

"Being soul mates."

My breath caught—words. I used to know words. In multiple languages, no less, but now all ability to speak vanished as I struggled to digest the information. Soul mates.

Cris regained his ability to speak first. "Thank you, Ms. Williams. We are in your debt."

"English, hon," I reminded.

"It's okay, I speak Spanish." Anne smiled dryly. "I accept payment in rare books. Normal books, not spell books. I wouldn't want to loot your library."

Cris nodded. "I will find something appropriate and see that it is sent to you."

"Can you let Patience know that we can start tomorrow?" I asked. "We're going to be busy tonight."

"Very busy," Cris added.

"Understood." Anne chuckled. "Have fun, kids."

We fled the office and shut the door behind us, and Cris promptly pulled me into an aisle and kissed me senseless.

"I love you," I said when I came up for air.

"I love you, my Natividad."

"All yours," I said. "Forever."

## ABOUT THE AUTHOR

Robyn Bachar writes romance with swords, sorcery, spaceships and submersibles. Bachar's novels feature action and adventure, danger and suspense, found families and happily ever afters. Her books have finaled twice in the PRISM Contest for Published Authors, twice in the Passionate Plume Contest, and twice in the EPIC eBook Awards.


facebook.com/AuthorRobynBachar
twitter.com/RobynBachar
instagram.com/robynbachar
bookbub.com/authors/robyn-bachar
amazon.com/author/robynbachar
goodreads.com/iamtherobyn

# OTHER TITLES BY ROBYN BACHAR

**The Galactic Cold War Trilogy**

**Sci-Fi Romance**

*Firefly meets James Bond in this action-adventure romance set in an alternate future where the Cold War never ended...*

Relaunch Mission

Contingency Plan

End Transmission

**Just One Spell Series**

**Fantasy Romance**

*Just one spell can change their fates...*

The Sephra's Tear

The Timefreeze Curse

**Bad Witch: The Emily Chronicles**

**Historical Paranormal Romance**

*Magic, matchmaking and murder!*

The Importance of Being Emily

Poison in the Blood

**Bad Witch Series**

**Paranormal Romance**

*Bad witches get things done.*

Blood, Smoke and Mirrors

Bloodlines and Broomsticks

Bewitched, Blooded and Bewildered

Blood, Toil and Trouble

Fire in the Blood

Bad Blood

Blood, Book and Candle

The Bloody End

**Cy'ren Rising Series**

**Sci-Fi Erotic Romance**

*Sci-fi romance so steamy it will fire your engines into overdrive.*

Nightfall

Morningstar

Sunsinger

**This Apocalypse Bites**

**Erotic Paranormal Romance**

*It sucks to be a vampire at the end of the world.*

Bite Me

*Read on for an excerpt from*
*Blood, Book and Candle*
*the next book in Robyn Bachar's*
***Bad Witch series***

*A love worth dying for...twice?*

Anne Williams is a seer—the rarest, most dangerous kind of magician—gifted with the ability to divine the past, present and future. Anne spent her life hiding her true nature to protect her from those who would abuse her prophetic powers, but with an impending apocalypse on the horizon Anne can't afford to stay in the shadows. Anne steps up the plate to help magiciankind, but someone tries to take her out of the game--permanently.

Wounded and with nowhere else to go, Anne finds shelter with chronicler Simon St. Jerome, but with one touch he plunges Anne into a tangled web of secrets and lies. Simon spent centuries concealing his past while recording the history of magician society, but nothing can hide the truth from a seer. As his soul mate, Anne is determined to discover every secret he's buried—including the tale of how she died once before in a failed attempt to spend eternity with her immortal lover.

As danger closes in around them, Anne and Simon must overcome the scars of their pasts, or risk never seeing their futures.

*Enjoy the following excerpt for* Blood, Book and Candle.

~

A bullet punched through the glass door of the Dusty Tomes as I flipped the sign to Closed. I stumbled from the impact, tripped on the hem of my broomstick skirt and fell. My head hit the hardwood floor with a loud thunk as screaming pain erupted from the wound and rushed through my body.

*New pain.* It'd been a while since I'd discovered a new pain, and my brain blanked in stunned surprise. I was an expert in both magical and mundane pain, but *this*—I hissed through clenched teeth and winced at the ceiling. This was a craptastic time for a new experience.

And to add insult to injury, I knew there'd be psychic jokes if I lived. *Oh, if you can see the future, why didn't you duck?* Sadly I'd experienced zero magical warning bells before the shot slammed into my shoulder, so I was really damn surprised.

"*Anne.*" Grandpa slammed the cash register drawer shut.

I gulped enough air to order him to get down, and Grandpa dropped behind the counter for cover. I grunted in pain as I rolled to a kneeling position and drew the pistol from the holster concealed in my boot.

I hadn't expected to get shot, but I'd been prepared for a fight for the past few weeks. Nearly half of the local magician population had vanished as though they'd been snaptured by a malevolent being—and in a way they had been. A relentless group of hunters who were part of something called Task Force Prometheus had been plaguing the local magician population for months. The Prometheans kidnapped some magicians and killed those they didn't deem useful to their evil plans to dissect us to learn how magic made us tick. We hadn't been hunted on this scale for centuries—few people believed in magic when science could explain most of the things that went bump in the night. We'd gotten comfortable. Lazy. And as a result, we were seriously unprepared when these assholes arrived. It had only been a matter of time before the hunters showed up at our store. Librarians were easy prey, and seers even more so.

Several more shots pierced the glass of the front display window, and I returned fire. Two shots—enough to let the hunters know I wasn't going without a fight, while still conserving my bullets. I'd become enough of a gun nut to shop the "concealed carry for her" catalogue for my boots, but not enough to spring for undergarments with spare ammo clips. That was definitely being added to my Christmas list.

Grandpa emerged from behind the counter and crawled across the floor—that had to be hell on his knees—and I scooted back to meet him. Fresh flashes of pain assaulted my senses with each move, like microeruptions following a volcano's big blast. I breathed through them just like I'd been taught—*steady, even, inhale through the nose, exhale through the mouth. You got this.*

"Stay down," I said.

"Dear gods." Grandpa reached for my wound in reflex but paused as he remembered the primary rule of seer club—never touch a seer without permission. It's such a joy being a seer—unlike every other kind of magician, I have no offensive or defensive magic, just prophetic visions and other fun psychic party tricks that make my life hell. Visions can be triggered by touch, especially from contact from another magician. The last thing I needed was his attempt at first aid sending me into a shrieking prophecy seizure. One of us had to be the tough one here, and no offense to my grandpa, but like most librarians his magical skill set was built for research and not combat. Because magic wouldn't protect me, I'd spent years learning mundane methods of self-defense.

"It's not bad," I said. "I'm okay."

"I think it went right through," Grandpa said.

"Of course it did." I grimaced and shifted my grip on my gun. In the grand scheme of things a bullet wound wasn't the worst of our problems. Magicians heal faster than mere mortals, and any magician worth their salt can handle a simple healing spell. My healing spells might be limited, but they are on point. They need to be, considering my extracurricular activities. I chanted the rhyming couplet to my strongest spell and the pain dialed down to something manageable.

"Don't worry," I said. "Head for the office. I'll cover you."

"Where did you get that thing?" He frowned at the gun, but I shook my head.

"Never mind. Go!"

We stayed low and scuttled past aisles of bookshelves —*Alchemy, Astrology, Divination, Numerology, Spellwork for Beginners.* The shop is sort of a running joke in our family, because we're real magicians who operate a bookstore that specializes in metaphysical mumbo jumbo geared toward the nonmagical majority. No amount of study could teach magic to someone who wasn't born with it in their blood and bone. I paused and leaned against the last row—*Witchcraft and Wizardry*—and adjusted my shooting stance as Grandpa struggled to open the door to the back room.

"It's locked," he said.

"What? I didn't lock it." And I knew he hadn't, either. "Try a knock spell."

Something crashed through the storefront's window, and with a whoosh flames carpeted the wooden floor. I spat several four-letter words as my heart raced with panic. It wasn't possible—we had so many wards against fire cast on this place that smokers on the sidewalk outside couldn't light up. Then again we knew there were demons hidden in the hunters' ranks, pulling the humans' strings for their own nefarious purposes, because apparently a shadowy, well-funded hunter organization hadn't been terrifying enough on its own. A couple of humans with guns I could deal with, but if a demon lurked outside we were in trouble.

"Got it." Grandpa yanked the door open only to find the back room also ablaze, and he cursed and slammed the door shut.

Panic choked my throat and I forced each steadying breath. Usually I'm the soul of self-control—seers are bombarded by noisy energy, and I have to keep calm and carry on or I'd be in a constant state of overloaded hysteria. I embraced the steady beat of pain throbbing in my shoulder and used the rhythm to concentrate.

"Why aren't the sprinklers working?" I asked.

The hungry flames spread to the first row of shelves, and the air filled with heat and smoke. We're fanatical about fire prevention because a bookstore's essentially a big pile of kindling. Spellcraft aside, there should've been alarms and a downpour by now, but instead the fire flared into an inferno.

"Not sure," he replied. "Maybe someone shut off the water."

"Well, I'm sending a strongly worded letter to the Village of Naperville later." I reached into my skirt pocket, tugged my phone free and clumsily unlocked it, only to discover that I had no bars and no Wi-Fi. "Son of a—"

"I can get to the phone up front," Grandpa said.

"Not through that." I shoved the phone back in my pocket. Fire leaped from the first to the second row, a vivid reminder that I didn't have a lot of time to ponder our next move. We needed backup. "I'll call Aunt Emily,"

"Your phone—"

I shook my head. "I'll *call* to her. She'll hear me."

His brow furrowed. "Have you done that before?"

"No, but there's a first time for everything." My "aunt" Emily was a seer, or at least she had been in life. I inherited my magic from her—the first of her descendants in several generations to be burdened with her curse. Lucky me. She could rescue us if I got through to her telepathically. Provided she could find a way in, because it was too bright for her to shadow step.

"I'll call her," I said. "You give them darkness to travel through."

Grandpa nodded, lurched to his feet and grabbed a heavy hardcover book. He swung at the florescent bulbs above our heads and they showered us with hot glass. I wasn't going to argue—a few glass shards were nothing compared to a bullet. He moved to the next fixture, and I closed my eyes and pictured Aunt Emily. The thick waves of brunette hair that hung long down her back, the affection in her warm gray eyes and the fair porcelain complexion that probably hadn't seen the sun since Victoria was queen. Family was everything to Aunt Emily. She was an immortal matriarch who watched over her descendants, and she would move heaven and earth like an avenging angel to protect what was hers.

My lungs itched and burned from the smoke, and the blood loss drained my magical batteries. After several agonizing moments Aunt Emily's mind brushed mine like phantom fingers patting my cheek. I clung to the connection with a jumbled reply filled with pain, blood and fire. The contact broke and I opened my eyes. Grandpa crouched beside me, and his face was etched with concern.

"Hang in there, honey. We'll be okay."

I didn't need to be a seer to know that he was lying. Bookstores and fire don't mix. Our life's work was turning to ash around us, and there was nothing we could do to save it, or ourselves.

My arms shook from the effort of keeping the gun trained on the front of the store—too many monsters were immune to fire to risk lowering my weapon. Fortunately even supernatural beings weren't immune to bullets. Any demons on the other side of the blaze were going to be greeted with a hail of gunfire—it wouldn't banish them, but it'd hurt enough to make them think twice.

"Let me take that," Grandpa said.

"No. You don't have firearms training."

He sighed and coughed. "How hard can it be? Point and shoot, right?"

"Not even a bit."

My aim dipped as my mental shields splintered. Too much stimuli and drama without enough magic to go around. Grandpa's fear doused me like a bucket of ice water, and I gasped and erupted into a coughing fit. Whispering thoughts from the surrounding suburb pressed against the edges of my mind, an inexorable invasion like a lava flow meandering to the sea.

I counted heartbeats until my senses zeroed in on a trio of beings approaching the entrance. No magic to speak of, and their thoughts were calm and calculating—not civilians. Hunters. A dark malevolence lurked behind them, farther away. Must be the demon giving them marching orders.

The hunters kicked in the door and I drew on my magic, inhaled, aimed, exhaled, and fired. The bullet stuck the lead man in the throat—right in the weak spot between his armored vest and helmet—and he dropped.

Aunt Emily emerged from the shadows Grandpa had created in the aisle next to us, with Uncle Michael close on her heels.

"Incoming," I snapped. A splash of energy from their entrance bombarded my connection to the attackers, and I abandoned supernatural aim in favor of emptying my weapon in the bad guys' general direction. When no one returned fire I holstered my empty gun. "I think I got them. Or at least discouraged them."

"What happened? Where did you get that?" Aunt Emily's eyes were wide, and her anxiety pricked my skin like I'd angered a nest of fire ants. Their faces and clothing were both smudged with smoke, and I frowned. I'd seen them shadow step before so I knew it wasn't a side effect of their shortcut through the shadow realm. Something was really rotten in Denmark.

"Anne's been shot. There's fire at both exits," Grandpa said.

Uncle Michael gave me a quick glance-over. "May I?"

"I can walk. Probably," I said.

"Not through the shadow realm," he said. "Particularly not with a bleeding wound."

"Right. One sec." I braced my mental shields and nodded, and he picked me up like a child about to be sent to bed. His energy was calm and solid—the family patriarch and unshakeable center. "Aunt" and "Uncle" were misnomers meant to hide their immortal natures, because the pair didn't appear old enough to be anyone's grandparents, much less several levels of great grandparents. Aunt Emily continued to radiate itchy irritation. She'd always been over-protective—she fussed over me on a good day, so she had to be half out of her mind right now.

He turned to Aunt Emily. "We'll take them to Simon."

"*No.*" Aunt Emily's horror was a gust of autumn wind that cut through the stifling heat.

"What?" Uncle Michael's brow furrowed with confusion, and I echoed the sentiment. Any port in a storm, right? Even a port owned by a salty old chronicler.

"Not to Simon's," she said. "Anywhere but there."

"Our options are limited," he said. "We obviously can't take them home."

*Weird.* I'd pry, but any seer snooping on my part would only end in me convulsing and speaking in tongues. "Decide fast," I said. "There's a demon outside, and I bet he has friends."

She scowled but nodded. "Very well. Simon's it is. Here, Arthur, lean on me." She took Grandpa's arm and they stepped into the shadows.

Uncle Michael carried me toward the darkness, and I squeezed my eyes shut and buried my face against his chest. I'd never been to the shadow realm, but I was sure I didn't want to see what was in it. The heat and crackle of the flames vanished, replaced by cold, eerie silence. An icy breeze tugged at the ends of my short-cropped hair, and I shivered. I had no idea where we were going, or how long it was going to take to get there, but I hoped it'd be a quick trip.

The cold vanished and I was warm again.

"What happened?" an unfamiliar voice asked. Maybe it was the mysterious Simon—I was probably the only one in my family who'd never met him. But I was also the only member of my family who wasn't a librarian, so I had no reason to cross his path. Magicians were cliquish that way. Being a seer was rather like being the new girl in high school, desperately searching for somewhere to sit at lunch while all the other groups of magicians declared that I couldn't sit with them.

"Our home was attacked, as was the store," Michael said. "The children are injured. Anne's been shot, she'll need a healer."

*Children.* Please. I was over thirty, and Grandpa was over eighty, but that must seem young to someone over a century old.

"Set her here," the speaker said.

Uncle Michael settled me into a chair, and someone poked the hole in my shoulder. I opened my eyes and a stranger loomed over me. Simon, presumably, judging by his calm, cold energy. Chronicler auras always felt chilly, as though they were encased in chunks of magical ice the moment they became immortal. But a chronicler should definitely be well versed enough in magician society to know the rules of interacting with a seer.

"Hey! Don't touch," I said.

Simon met my gaze. He had the palest, most piercing blue eyes I'd ever seen, and my breath caught. There was something familiar about those eyes... The dizzy twist of the room was the only warning I had before the vision hit.

As always, my magic had terrible timing.

I screamed as I spasmed and seized, caught in the throes of uncontrolled magic. The voices around me faded, and I could barely hear them even though they were shouting—*She's going into shock! I'll get the potions. We need to stop the bleeding...her pulse is fading...*

My skin felt as though it was covered in a thick sheet of ice, and my entire body was leaden. I lay atop a wooden table, my arms and legs too heavy to move. My head was turned to the side, and I recognized the familiar claustrophobia of being surrounded by tightly packed bookcases crowding the room. The library didn't grant its usual comfort, and I stared at the fire in a nearby hearth. The fire was dying, which seemed appropriate, as so was I.

Dying by gasps and small degrees—at first the blood rushed from my veins and I hurtled toward the point where the spell would catch me and make me immortal. Or should have, rather, if it had worked. Instead the magic had ground to a halt, and darkness crept in around me like the roll of evening fog. My long golden hair fanned out beside me on the table, the firelight giving it a dull sheen.

*Long hair*...this was a vision. My hair had been short for the past few months. Maybe it was a vision of the future, but it felt more like a memory—recorded and scripted, beyond my control. It wasn't a memory of mine. I'd already had one near-death experience, and it was permanently seared into my brain as one of the top ten things I'd never forget, not to mention permanently scarred across my skin.

"Darling, look at me. I need you to drink again." The voice was distant—far away, as though my love was standing across a ballroom instead of hovering anxiously at my side. The faintness filled me with sorrow as I realized there would be no forever for us now. I would die, and he would likely follow from the grief of it. Most soul mates did, unable to continue after the loss when the broken bond left a gaping metaphysical wound in the surviving partner. The ritual had been meant to spare him from that loss—I was mortal, and my love was not. But the ritual had failed.

"I can't. It's not working. You have to let me go." I wanted to sound strong, resolute, but the words were difficult because I was exhausted, and I struggled to force them past my lips.

"*No.* The spell will work, I know it will. Now *drink.*"

I licked my lips and recognized the lingering coppery taste of blood. Was I—or she, rather—a chronicler? Uncle Michael was a chronicler—a librarian who served the Order of St. Jerome as an immortal records keeper sustained by the blood of living magicians. Unless I was a necromancer. They were blood drinkers, too, but they sought immortality for selfish reasons. No purpose, just greed and endless hunger. My mind rebelled at the idea of being that evil, and I latched on to the assurance that because I was in a library I must be a chronicler. Or at least I was trying to become one. The ritual had something like a fifty percent success rate, maybe less. Immortality wasn't easy.

"No," I repeated. "It's over. I'm sorry."

My heavy eyelids slid shut and I waited to drift off into a final sleep, but cold fingers on the side of my face turned my head. Blinking my eyes open, I looked up at the face of my soul mate. He had the palest, most piercing blue eyes I'd ever seen.

*Blood, Book and Candle is available everywhere books are sold.*

# BAD WITCH GLOSSARY

*alchemist*: a magician who specializes in brewing potions. The source of the magic is not the ingredients themselves—though they can help add an extra kick—but the alchemist who infuses her own magic into a potion. Alchemists are the most mercenary magicians because their magic is the most marketable.

*chronicler*: a librarian who has joined the Order of St. Jerome and become a vampire. Chroniclers undergo a ritual that was originally stolen from the necromancers and altered. It stops their aging and places the body in a sort of stasis. Like the original ritual, there is a chance of failure, and the odds of survival are only thirty to forty percent. To survive, chroniclers ingest magic by consuming the blood of living magicians and often take blood as payment for their services. Chroniclers are responsible for recording magician history and archiving spells and magical research. *See also* Order of St. Jerome.

*Council of Three*: a magician governing body. Every type of magician is monitored/ruled over by a Council of Three, as are faeries. There are levels to councils—regional, national, global, etc.

*demon*: an entity native to one of the hell realms. Unlike other magical creatures, demons cannot be killed, only banished back to their realm. However, if a magician travels to that realm, he or she can kill the demon there. Physical attacks on people in "haunted" houses are caused by demonic entities (ghosts can't physically interact with their surroundings). Demons come in a variety of shapes and sizes due to the difference in hells—some embody sins or vices, others natural elements like faeries, and some are just outright nightmarish bogeymen.

*faerie*: one of the magical races formerly native to Earth. Faeries are extremely long-lived, but are not immortal. In many ways they are embodiments of magic, the different clans representing different aspects and elements of it. Faeries left Earth and created their own world after the extinction of the elves, but that act left them damaged as a species, unable to reproduce with each other. A full-blooded faerie has not been born since the formation of their world. Many magicians owe their magic to their faerie heritage.

*favor*: a magical debt owed to a demon or summoner. Favors are no small matter, and are granted in exchange for powerful magic. A mark representing the favor is tattooed into the skin of the magician who owes it, and the mark disappears once the favor is repaid.

*guardian*: an enforcer of magical law and order. They work for the higher powers to ensure criminals are apprehended, but councils are responsible for judging guilt or innocence. Guardians can be called on to execute the guilty, if necessary.

*hunter*: an individual or group who hunts and kills magicians. Some hunters have personal reasons, such as having a family member killed by shapeshifters. Others do it for sport, believing magicians to be challenging prey.

*kinslayer*: a magician or magical being who has murdered a member of his/her family. Magicians have always been outnumbered by straights, and after the elves became extinct great importance was placed upon preserving the remaining races. Killing other magicians is frowned upon, but it is considered a great crime to kill a member of one's own family. Kinslayers are often socially ostracized by other magicians.

*librarian*: a magician specializing in history and research.

Because they study a variety of magics, librarians can cast any type of spell. However, when a librarian casts them, these spells are less powerful. Example, a sorcerer's fireball is less like a softball and more like a golf ball if a librarian casts it. Most librarians aspire to serve the Order of St. Jerome. Though few are chosen to become chroniclers, many work as servants or assistants. *See also* chronicler; Order of St. Jerome.

*magician*: a person with magic in their blood. Most magicians have inherited their magic from faerie relatives, but in the past many humans were born with their own innate magic. This dwindled over time as magic faded from this world. Only people with magic in their blood can cast magic. No amount of equipment or materials will allow a straight to cast magic.

*necromancer*: a practitioner of death magic. Necromancers specialize in dealing with ghosts, zombies, and other icky dead things. When a magician becomes a necromancer he is apprenticed to a master, and once his training is complete he undergoes a ritual to become a master himself (*see* vampire). This ritual is risky, with a roughly fifty percent chance of failure. Master necros build up bad karma for jamming a spoke in the wheel of life, and when a master dies horrible things happen to his soul.

*oathbreaker*: a magician known to have broken an official oath. Sworn oaths are taken very seriously in magician society. If a person swears to do something, such as fulfill a quest or take on a sacred responsibility, failure to uphold the oath can result in social ostracism. Oathbreakers are considered untrustworthy, and few people agree to deal with them.

*Oberon*: an ambassador responsible for overseeing relations between Earth and Faerie (if the position is held by a woman, she is referred to as a *Titania*). An Oberon or Titania maintains balance between faerie and magician society within a region on Earth, ensuring that faeries do not cause too much mischief within that region, and that the local magicians do not abuse their access to Faerie.

*Order of St. Jerome*: the organization of chroniclers. The order was founded by a group who decided that having immortal librarians to protect magician records and be able to remember stories and events was necessary to maintain a record of magician history. The necromancers were furious that their ritual for creating immortality had been stolen, but a war between the two factions was prevented when the order agreed not to become involved in magician politics. The group has gone through many names over the years, but St. Jerome is the most recent and longest lasting.

*seer*: a magician who can read auras and receive prophetic visions. Seers are the rarest kind of magician, with only a handful in the entire world. Their visions center around the person they're reading or a traumatic event in an area. Seers are not mediums, and though they can get a feeling for the energy in a house, they don't communicate with the dead—because that's necromancer territory. Seers are particularly adept at locating a person's soul mate.

*shadowspawn*: a faerie who has been expelled from Faerie for evil acts. Though faeries have a high tolerance for mischief, they do have limits as to the sort of crimes allowed in and outside of Faerie. Faeries convicted of acts of great evil are expelled from Faerie, banished to live on Earth.

*shadow realm*: a hell dimension. The shadow realm exists in an eternal state of twilight, where the landscape, buildings and demon inhabitants are made of darkness. Vampires and shadowspawn faeries use the shadow realm as a shortcut to travel between places on Earth that are steeped in darkness. *See also* shadowspawn; shadowstep; vampire.

*shadowstep*: a method of transportation used by master necromancers, chroniclers and shadowspawn faeries. To keep vampires from causing mayhem in other worlds, the higher powers closed the doors to them—except for the hell dimensions. Shadowspawn faeries and vampires brave or foolish enough to make the trip can travel through the shadow realm.

*shapeshifter*: a magician infected with wild magic and possessing an animal spirit. The most common shifters are canine, with the rest made up of feline, ursine, equine and avian. Shifters coexist with their animal, almost like having a split personality, and can shift into a hybrid animal/human form and the full animal form. Many shifters, particularly predators, revel in their beast, which has led to shifters being considered subhuman by other magicians and even hunted by sorcerers. *See also* wild magic.

*sorcerer*: a magician specializing in elemental magic typically destructive in nature. Like witches, sorcerers use elemental magic, and tend to focus on one element in particular. In general their magic does not require spoken spells or physical ingredients; large, formal rituals are rare occurrences. Sorcerers are the magicians most likely to become necromancers, as well as being most likely to be kept as a necromancer's pet.

*soul mate*: a soul's perfect match. Soul mates are not always romantic partners and can be represented in other close relationships, such as best friends. Because souls are reincarnated, a person can meet his or her soul mate in several lives, or none at all. Also, due to free will soul mates are not guaranteed true love or a happily ever after. Seers can be helpful in finding a person's soul mate.

*straights*: a slang term for nonmagicians. There are many other terms, such as *voids*.

*summoner*: a magician dealing in summoning, binding, and/or banishing magical entities. Summoners capture and bind their prey, trading magical favors or power in exchange for release. They mainly deal in demons, but with the right information, such as a True Name, they can deal with any living entity—elementals, imps or faeries. Dealing with demons is risky business and wears on a summoner over time. They begin to take on demonic physical traits and may even become demons themselves, at which point they are often pulled into a hell dimension that becomes their new home.

*Task Force Prometheus*: a secret government project researching magicians and magic; also known as *hunters* or *Methees* (slang).

While looking for terrorists, the government uncovered the hidden society of magicians. A top-secret task force was formed to study magic-users, to find the source of their magic in order to weaponize it.

*Titania*: an ambassador responsible for overseeing relations between Earth and Faerie (if the position is held by a man, he is referred to as an *Oberon*). An Oberon or Titania maintains balance between faerie and magician society within a region on Earth, ensuring that faeries do not cause too much mischief within that region, and that the local magicians do not abuse their access to Faerie.

*True Name*: the name of a magician or magical being that has power over that person. In modern society, names aren't given as much weight and a magician's True Name holds little to no power. It is considered rude to use a magician's True Name, especially without permission. The names of older beings, such as demons, faeries and vampires, can still hold power and be used against them. Faeries in particular guard their True Names jealously and go by a number of pseudonyms.

*vampire*: a slang term for a master necromancer or chronicler. *Vampire* is considered rude by many older master necros and chroniclers. They do, however, share some traits with the popular vampire myth. They must feed on the blood of living magicians—specifically on the magic within the blood—to maintain their existence. Most keep spouses, partners, or "pets" as blood sources. It is extremely rare for a vampire to kill during feeding (when you're done milking the cow, you don't slaughter it).

*wild magic*: a form of magic originating from an animal, known to be unpredictable. Most magicians consider shapeshifters to be *infected* with wild magic. This magic imbues its host with the spirit of the animal it originated from, and it also interferes with the host's original magic. Most magicians fear being infected with wild magic.

*witch*: a magician specializing in elemental magic, focused on healing and self-defense. Witches have a strict policy of doing no harm with their magic, which makes them unique among other magicians. Witches like ritual with their magic, using elaborate spells that require special tools, spoken words and physical ingredients.

www.ingramcontent.com/pod-product-compliance
Lightning Source LLC
LaVergne TN
LVHW010614100826
845148LV00014B/2964

* 9 7 8 1 7 3 3 5 7 6 1 1 6 *